Web of Deception

Jane Peart

Fleming H. Revell
A Division of Baker Book House Co
Grand Rapids, Michigan 49516

© 1996 by Jane Peart

Published by Fleming H. Revell
a division of Baker Book House Company
P.O. Box 6287, Grand Rapids, MI 49516-6287

Third printing, October 1996

Printed in the United States of America

Library of Congress Cataloging-in-Publication Data

Peart, Jane.
    Web of deception / Jane Peart.
      p. cm.
    ISBN 0-8007-5598-7 (paper)
      1. Young women—England—Fiction. 2. Governesses—England—Fiction. I. Title.
    PS3566.E238W4 1996
    813'.54—dc20   95-49284

Web of Deception

Prologue

Havelock Hall Academy for Young Ladies

April 1875

Excuse me, miss. This just come for you."

Rachel Penniston looked up from the composition papers she was correcting to see Annie, the school's maid, standing at the door of the teachers' study. She was holding out a yellow envelope.

"For *me?*" Rachel asked, startled. She had never received one before, but she knew a telegram usually brought bad news of some sort. Word of some disaster. An accident. An illness. Death!

"For *me?*" Rachel repeated. "You're *sure?*"

"Yes, miss," Annie repeated. "Miss Huddleston told me to bring it to you."

At the mention of the headmistress's name, Rachel knew it was no mistake. She replaced her pen into the inkwell and held out her suddenly clammy hand for the telegram Annie thrust toward her. The maid rubbed her hands on her apron, as if glad to be rid of the ominous thing, and scurried out of the room.

Shakily Rachel tore it open and with unbelieving eyes read the news of her father's fatal heart attack.

The next few hours were a blur. The sympathetic headmistress told Rachel that of course she must leave at once. There were only two more weeks until the term's end, and her classes could be divided up among the other teachers. She must not worry about anything.

Still dazed, Rachel found herself on the train journeying home. Her mind seemed numb. How fragile happiness was, how quickly it could be shattered. Only this morning she had been happily thinking that soon she would be going home to the vicarage for the summer holiday. Now, instead, she would be attending her father's funeral.

The closer she got to Meadowmead, the more Rachel understood that the life she had taken for granted all these years had come to an end. Her father had been vicar there since she was a little girl. They had come there following her mother's death when Rachel was three years old. She had lived there until she had gone away to boarding school at Havelock Hall as a student for three years, as a teacher for the last two. Except for school, Rachel had led the sheltered life of a minister's daughter in a quiet country village. All that was over. What lay ahead for her now, she had no idea.

*T*hree weeks later, seated at her small, slanted desk in the alcoved window of the sitting room, Rachel was writing replies to the many condolence notes she'd received. Pausing for a moment, she became aware of an unusual flurry of scrubbing, sweeping, and polishing going on around her. The smells of soap, starch, and lemon wax permeated the air. The funeral hardly over, Fanny Dilsworth, the housekeeper, was doing a thorough house cleaning. It seemed curious because the house had shone and sparkled for the funeral reception. Why was she at it again? Slowly, it made sense. Fanny was making sure everything would be immaculate for the next occupants of the vicarage.

For as long as Rachel could remember Fanny had been their housekeeper. It had not occurred to Rachel that Fanny was the *vicarage* housekeeper. Her salary was paid by the church.

As this realization came slowly to Rachel, so did the fact that the house they had called home all these years was church property. It would become the residence of the new vicar, yet to be appointed. Of course, Fanny hoped to retain her position. All this activity was designed to impress the new vicar's family.

For the first time since her father had died, Rachel understood that she had not only become an orphan, but homeless as well.

She was now completely alone in the world and almost penniless. Her father lived what he preached. He gave most of his small income away to the poor. All Rachel had was a small inheritance from her mother to be paid when she reached the age of twenty-one. That was a year away. Nothing else but her small teacher's salary. As the youngest, newest one on staff, hers had also been the lowest. It was barely enough to take care of her personal needs. Without her father's support, what would she do?

Becoming a teacher had been mostly happenstance for Rachel. From an early age her father had taught her not just the basic 3-Rs but the subjects in which he himself was interested. Even when she was a student, the headmistress at Havelock recognized Rachel had been educated beyond most and had her tutor some of the slower girls. Eventually Rachel was offered a teaching post. With no other plans at the time, Rachel agreed, happy to have some spending money. She was given board and room, and her school holidays were spent at home at the vicarage in the beautiful countryside she loved. There she did mostly what she enjoyed, including helping her father with some of his translations.

She had never really planned a future for herself. Now, this was a necessity. But what? She found teaching tedious and boring at times. Rachel had an active imagination, a romantic nature, as well as an adventurous streak. Not knowing how she might accomplish it, she longed to travel and daydreamed of having a grand passion, a wildly romantic love. Preferably the object of that love would be a poet, a writer, or musician whose spirit would match hers and who would fall madly in love with her. That's as far as the fantasy ever went. How she would ever meet such a man, living the life she had, was beyond even her imagination. However, in her secret heart, Rachel had not abandoned hope that one day it would happen.

That dream seemed impossibly far away now. Watching Fanny scrub, polish, and wax, Rachel had to face reality, make some plans. The thought of returning to Havelock for another year of teaching was depressing as well as impractical. She doubted her salary would be increased. There must be ways she had never thought of that a poor gentlewoman could earn a living. Rachel had always supposed she would live with her father until something happened, perhaps that magical moment when a romantic suitor appeared on her horizon. She must forget such foolishness now and make some down-to-earth decisions.

She purchased a London newspaper the very next day and searched the HELP SOUGHT and POSITIONS AVAILABLE columns under the EMPLOYMENT section. She looked for ads beginning with such euphemisms as "refined young lady." Rachel was not sure exactly what she was hoping to find. How could she be? She had no experience.

She was beginning to feel a little desperate when she saw an ad that was not only plausible but intriguing.

ONE-YEAR EMPLOYMENT OPPORTUNITY. Seeking a well-educated young woman of refinement and accomplishment and schooled in social graces to serve as companion-governess to two motherless children, a boy age seven and a girl age nine, while their father is abroad. Although the residence is located in the country, it is on the London train line, and it has all the modern amenities, beautiful park-like grounds, a resident housekeeper and butler supervising a capable, well-trained household staff. Teaching experience helpful but not necessary. The main duty of the person chosen for this position will be to provide compassionate, caring companionship for the children. To arrange for a personal interview, please contact Mr. Brett Venable at Box 207, care of this paper.

After reading it over twice, Rachel decided this might be a real possibility. She liked children, got along fine with the little village tots who attended her Sunday school class, and enjoyed popularity with the younger pupils at Havelock Hall who were often sent off to boarding school at an early age and apt to be homesick. She would prefer to find work in the country than in a bustling, filthy city like London. It sounded an easy enough job with no other duties or responsibilities than to keep two small children happy.

Putting thought to action, Rachel wrote a letter of application in her best penmanship and posted it at once.

A week later she received a reply on paper with a London law firm's letterhead giving her a date and time to come for an interview. Astonished to receive so prompt a response she could not help but wonder what might have warranted so quick an answer—her stationery with the vicarage address or her character references from Havelock Hall's headmistress and the bishop who had confirmed her when she was twelve.

Regardless, she was gratified and prepared immediately to follow it up with a good impression at her personal interview. She wanted to present herself to the best advantage. What to wear for her appointment posed no real problem. She did not have a large wardrobe. Her newest dress was the simple black one she had worn for her father's funeral. She added a lace collar and small cameo pin to soften its starkness. Worn with her dove-gray caped coat and bonnet trimmed with black grosgrain ribbons, on the whole she was satisfied her outfit was appropriate and in good taste.

Having been brought up with the oft-repeated admonition that vanity was a sin and pride went before a fall, Rachel had no idea what a lovely young woman she was. In appearance she was slim enough to be graceful. Her complexion, the rosy one of a country girl, needed no artifice; her eyes were a clear brown, her soft brown hair glossy. Her manner had warmth and sincerity; her smile was sweet, her expression alert and intelligent. Friends loved Rachel for her generous spirit, her sense of humor, and her loyalty.

The following Monday, Rachel boarded the London bound train. She felt both nervous and excited. She had never done anything like this before. How should she act? Eager, reserved, enthusiastic, reticent? At length, she decided all she could do was be herself and hope that Mr. Venable liked her, felt he could trust her with his children. Rachel whispered a little prayer. She had always been taught to ask for only what was rightfully hers in her life. Following that precept, she was told, would eliminate fear, jealousy, or anger. Any work for which she had a natural call by gift or inclination was hers to do. If she held that attitude it would give her courage and faith. If the position with Mr. Venable's children was supposed to be hers, it would happen.

As the train pulled into the London station, Rachel stepped out onto the platform. The air was filled with the smell of cinders and oil, the clamor of compartment doors slamming, wheels of luggage carts, loud voices, and hurrying footsteps. Rachel's heart pounded excitedly. She stood there for a moment absorbing the bustle all around her. Then, feeling as though she were on the brink of a great adventure, Rachel moved into the crowds rushing toward the gates leading into the large terminal and pushed through the doors where hansom cabs were lined up outside the station. As if she had been doing it all her life, she held up her hand to indicate she needed one. As one drew up in front of her, she confidently gave the driver the address of the Morrison-Tolby law firm.

As they weaved their way through streets heavily trafficked with carriages, cabs, and delivery wagons, Rachel glanced from left to right. On every side large, impressive buildings rose, well-dressed men walked briskly along the sidewalks on their way to important businesses. They drove past stores with fashionable displays in the windows, past theaters and restaurants. Everywhere she looked some new interesting scene caught her attention. London was a far cry from the country town where she had grown up or even the slightly larger one of Sudsbury where Havelock Hall was located.

Once inside the law office, Rachel gave her name to the clerk at the reception desk then glanced around. It was impressive—richly furnished, deeply carpeted, darkly paneled. On the walls hung gold framed portraits of formidable gentlemen in robes and barrister wigs. Then from a hallway off to her left a tall man attired in a dark frock coat approached, hand extended.

"Miss Penniston? Good afternoon. I am Bradley Morrison, Brett Venable's attorney."

He had thick, iron gray hair and a long, solemn face, keen blue eyes regarding her intently from behind silver-rimmed spectacles.

"Won't you come into my office? Mr. Venable is waiting to meet you."

Rachel's heart thrummed as she accompanied Mr. Morrison down the hall. He opened a door for her into another impressive office. The man who rose to greet her had a direct gaze, firm handshake, and courteous manner. His lean build made him appear taller than he actually was. Although Rachel was tall for a girl, she noticed his candid, gray eyes were almost on a level with her own. His skin had the healthy look of a man who spent much time outdoors, probably on horseback. His features were nicely molded, regular, his mouth singularly controlled, giving his face strength and character.

With a gesture Mr. Morrison offered Rachel one of two comfortable leather armchairs, then took his place behind the mahogany desk. He turned to Mr. Venable as though indicating the interview should begin.

Taking that as his cue, Mr. Venable commenced pleasantly. "Tell me something about yourself, Miss Penniston, and why you think you might be interested in this position."

Rachel had always prided herself on being intuitive about people, and immediately something in Brett Venable's eyes and expression touched her. She couldn't say just what it was, but she had the feeling that, somehow, tragedy had marked him. The ad had used the word "motherless" in describing the children, so naturally he was a widower. Whether it had been a recent loss or something that had happened years before she had no way to know. Although he was outwardly composed, she saw a trace of melancholy in his deep-set eyes.

Rachel briefly sketched her background, thinking even to her own ears, it sounded rather bland and very simple. She probably did not have the depth of experience or wisdom a father would look for in the person who was to be with his children while he was on a long journey.

Next came questions about Rachel's education. Mr. Venable encouraged her to discuss her interests, which were, thanks to her father, varied and of wider than ordinary range. Especially for a girl. She noticed Venable's occasional nod or smile, as though he found her answers interesting.

"I'm not sure if I made it entirely clear that our home, Talisman, is quite isolated, no close neighbors, a good mile's walk from the village. There are no theaters, no shops of any consequence, none of the usual amusements a young lady of your age might be accustomed to enjoying. I want you to understand this so there will be no later regrets should you accept the position. Do you think such a lack of social activities would be too difficult for you?"

Given her own preferences and how limited her social opportunities had actually been, Rachel felt an irrepressible smile tug at her lips.

"Sir, you are asking a *vicar's* daughter?"

Her answer evidently amused him. A genuine smile broke across Mr. Venable's rather serious countenance.

"At Talisman we have a well-stocked library, as well as riding trails through the surrounding woodland and large gardens with walking paths. There are many other pursuits and pastimes to be found there for a reasonably resourceful person." He paused, frowning slightly. "However, I felt it necessary to make it clear that we are quite a distance from many commonly accepted amusements. Some might tend to get lonely or melancholy in so isolated a spot. I'll be a great deal too far away to make any substitution for my children's companion should she become unhappy, or worse, want to leave."

"I can assure you, sir, that would not happen with me. I love the country, the outdoors. I grew up an only child in a motherless home myself. I am skilled at amusing myself and find pleasure in solitary endeavors."

"Good! I hope you can understand why I have to make certain the person I employ will stay."

"Of course."

A silence fell. There was a tangible tenseness to it that made Rachel curious. Mr. Venable seemed to be pondering whether to ask something further. He exchanged two or three glances with Mr. Morrison, who gave a nearly imperceptible nod. Whatever question was asked and answered, some decision was made.

Mr. Venable seemed somewhat uncomfortable, then clearing his throat he asked, "You will forgive me, Miss Penniston, if this seems rather personal, but I'm sure you can understand my children's welfare is my first consideration, and assuring myself of all the circumstances surrounding them during my absence is of great concern to me. Therefore, if you will indulge my being quite frank, I feel it necessary to inquire if you are involved—how shall I phrase this?—do you have, at this time, any sort of understanding or commitment of a romantic nature with a person of the opposite sex that would interfere in any way or compete with your complete dedication to the care of my children?"

Mr. Venable shifted uneasily in his chair before continuing. "I could not allow any person not known to myself to come to Talisman as a visitor, nor could I countenance anyone in my employ entertaining callers of a social kind without my knowledge or acquaintance with those individuals.

In other words, Miss Penniston, if you are engaged to be married, or in any such arrangement, or if there is anyone you might have the occasion to see or have visit you while at Talisman, I must know. I cannot take the chance—well, you can see, I must have your commitment that if you are offered this position, and accept it, you would have no other interest but my children for the length of your employment."

Again Rachel suppressed a smile. She mentally reviewed her romantic possibilities. The pale curate who had been her father's assistant the summer before, her friend Emily's roly-poly cousin Alfred, who had been so *smitten* with her on her last visit he had tripped all over himself and croquet wickets in his pursuit, or perhaps Monsieur Deveraux, the pudgy, fortyish French teacher at school who had shown a certain unwanted interest.

"No, there is no one. I am not romantically involved with anyone." She answered truthfully, albeit with inner regret. That fantasy lover she had dreamed of so often had not appeared, nor was there much hope he would given her present situation. Certainly not if she were offered and accepted this job.

Mr. Venable looked satisfied. "Well, I think we have covered everything, Miss Penniston." He glanced again at his lawyer. "I should make it clear that you—that is, *anyone* selected for this position—would not have sole responsibility for the children. My late wife's sister, actually her half-sister, is coming from Canada to stay while I'm away."

He hesitated, as if debating whether it was necessary to explain more. "My trip to Australia is actually family business that concerns her. It is to settle some legal tangles over property of my late father-in-law, who was, of course, both my wife's and my sister-in-law's father. It is part of the estate willed to his two daughters. Eventually all will be inherited by my children, and this is too long and arduous a journey for my sister-in-law to undertake. Her health has not been of the best. She has a heart ailment, not life-threatening but serious enough she should not be subjected to the undue strain such a trip would involve."

He paused again, sighed. "She has, however, agreed to come to England and stay at Talisman while I'm gone. Unfortunately, her sailing date was unexpectedly changed, and she will not be arriving until after I have left. Time is of the essence in settling these matters in Australia. Because of this it seemed imperative I have someone at Talisman right away whose sole responsibility would be my children." He frowned. "I did understand correctly from your letter, didn't I, that you are available immediately?"

Thinking of the way Fanny Dilsworth was wielding the broom at the vicarage, Rachel guessed *she* would be the next thing Fanny would be relieved and happy to sweep out. Rachel nodded. "Yes."

"Good! Believe me, I don't look forward to being away from Delphine and Derrick, my children. I don't think I mentioned their names before, did I?" Venable's expression softened as he spoke about them. "They are wonderful children, bright, curious, and good humored. I suppose, like most parents, I am prejudiced. Since their mother's death when they were quite young, I have devoted my life to them. We spend a great deal of time together and are going to miss each other."

He sighed, and Rachel could tell his emotions were very close to the surface. "That is why I am especially concerned to have someone kind, sensitive, and gentle caring for them. Lessons are not as important to them right now as having a stable, responsible companion." He spoke emphatically, adding almost as an afterthought, "That is, of course, until Verdonia comes—their aunt—Verdonia Templeton."

At the name Verdonia Templeton, Rachel felt a strange little frisson, almost a shiver. Why, she didn't know. Had she heard the name somewhere before? Was she someone famous, perhaps? But the moment passed, and Mr. Venable was speaking. She leaned forward to listen.

"I hope to conclude my business in Australia within eight to ten months. However, I have allowed for unforeseen events that might prolong my stay there and have stipulated the length of employment as a year to allow for any unexpected delay."

At this point Mr. Morrison stood, leaned over his desk. "If you please, Mr. Venable, I believe Miss Penniston should be asked if she would be willing to sign a contract, a legal binding contract, agreeing to remain for the period of a full year."

Mr. Venable turned to Rachel. "Would you?"

Although Rachel had been brought up with the scriptural admonition "let your aye be aye, your nay be nay," she hesitated only slightly. This concerned father needed reassurance. It would be a kindness to comply with his request.

"Yes. Certainly."

Brett Venable got to his feet. "Thank you so much for coming, Miss Penniston. As you may realize, we have some other applicants we are obligated to interview, but I want to assure you this personal interview has confirmed for me the impression made by your excellent letter."

Rachel was aware of a cautionary gesture from Mr. Morrison, as if to warn Venable not to say anything more. A lawyerly movement to protect his client, she assumed, in case a better person presented herself to be interviewed. The lawyer came around from behind his massive desk and walked to Rachel's side to escort her to the door.

Rachel rose, thanked Mr. Venable, and offered her gloved hand.

He took it with a warm smile and firm clasp. "We'll be in touch with you, Miss Penniston, and thank you again for coming."

Rachel was escorted by Mr. Morrison's clerk to a cab, evidently called and paid for by the lawyer, waiting outside to take her to the train station. After settling herself comfortably, Rachel pondered the possibilities should she be hired by Mr. Venable.

Back on the train, Rachel had a compartment to herself and time to think. As the outside landscape changed from the grimy outskirts of the city to the rolling rural countryside, Rachel felt a gradual relaxing of tension. She thought back over the interview, of the questions she had been asked, her answers, her impression of Brett Venable. Somehow she especially recalled Mr. Venable saying, "I want to emphasize we are very isolated at Talisman."

What lay beneath that emphasis? Was there something he wasn't saying? Rachel felt a vague uneasiness, almost the same strange sensation she had felt at the mention of Verdonia Templeton's name.

Although she had liked Brett Venable very much, especially his forthrightness and his candor, there had been a reserve about him, something hidden, something held back.

Rachel also had the feeling Mr. Morrison had been somewhat uncomfortable throughout the interview. He seemed anxious that his client was being too open, talking too freely. Rachel also had the sense Mr. Venable had been ready to hire her on the spot. Maybe Mr. Morrison thought her too young, too inexperienced. Whatever *their* impression of *her,* Rachel had much to consider herself. She thought over the things they had discussed. Mr. Venable had been very honest about the situation. The isolation of his home, the lack of outside stimuli. Would she really want to spend an entire year in the company of two small children, a household of servants, without any people her own age, no intellectual or social exchange of any sort? Was that what she really wanted?

Rachel looked out the window at the passing landscape. Everything was becoming more familiar—rosy stone cottages nestled in the valleys, sheep grazing on the hillside. She would soon be back in Meadowmead. If the Venable job were offered her and she accepted, it would mean stepping into an entirely new world, a different life.

Meadowmead was a market town, the center for many smaller villages surrounding it. It was a friendly place with community events, such as garden fetes and fairs, amateur theatricals, and concerts throughout the year. Rachel also had friends from her school days and often spent weekend visits at their homes.

From Mr. Venable's descriptions, Craigburne, the small town on the Cornish coast where Talisman was located, had no such social occasions, or at least none he was aware of or in which he participated. He apparently led a lonely widower's life there except for the company of his son and daughter. And expected her to be content to do the same.

It was certainly something to consider.

Rachel, fun-loving and outgoing, had been the youngest on the staff of teachers at Havelock. She had a more romantic and adventurous spirit than the others and had found she had to suppress some of her spontaneity in their company. Her holidays were the only thing that had kept her from feeling too trapped among the rather staid group of teachers, most of them spinsters. Sometimes she feared she might end up the same way.

Perhaps taking the position Mr. Venable outlined would be a mistake. Acceptance meant she'd be shutting herself off for a full year from the chance of meeting anyone.

Maybe she should take a little more time, explore some other possibilities, look for a job with more social advantages. Not that she *knew* for sure Venable had decided to hire her.

By the time her train reached Meadowmead, Rachel had just about decided to turn down the Venable job if it were offered. However, as luck would have it, that decision was taken out of her hands. Or at least badly jolted. Upon her arrival at the vicarage, she found a very excited Fanny Dilsworth. While Rachel was in London, the newly appointed vicar and his wife had come to inspect the house. They were scheduled to take possession within a month.

Shaken by this news Rachel studied the POSITIONS OFFERED column in the next day's newspaper with a renewed sense of urgency. She quickly exhausted the potential employment opportunities, such as they were. She checked them off one by one—a clerk in a bookbinding shop, an assistant to a milliner, a secretary to a veteran of the Crimean War, to organize his military records and write his memoirs. None of these sounded as attractive as the job described by Brett Venable. Perhaps the most important consideration was that the salary he had offered far exceeded the ones listed. Beggars couldn't be choosers, Rachel told herself. In her situation, she had to be practical.

The more she thought about it, a year at a luxurious country estate and two amiable children to look after was a far better prospect than the others. Even the name Talisman was intriguing. She would like to have asked how it came to be called that, but naturally she had not felt free to ask.

*R*achel found herself hoping she *would* be offered the position of companion-governess for the children at Talisman. For the next ten days she made frequent trips to the postbox at the end of the vicarage garden, hoping for a letter from Brett Venable.

Fanny Dilsworth's daily efforts to get the house in readiness for the new arrivals made Rachel more and more uncomfortable. So it was with elation she finally received a letter with an embossed crest postmarked from Craigburne. In a bold, slanted hand Brett Venable wrote, "Of all the candidates interviewed, we feel your qualifications warranted offering you the position. We would like you to come two weeks before my departure, May 10th. Please let us know the day and time of your train's arrival, and you will be met at the Craigburne station."

Rachel shared the news she would be leaving within the week with Fanny, who tried not to show too much relief at this announcement. Rachel was amused. Fanny had been anxious to get on with her cleaning and had left Rachel's room until last.

There was little enough for Rachel to pack. Simplicity had been her father's way of life, and Rachel's accumulations were surprisingly few. A few treasured books, daguerreotypes of her parents, a book of pressed flowers she had collected. Her father had been a botanist and taught her to enjoy rare plants and herbs. In a way, it was a kind of journal of their walks together in the surrounding woods, a precious memory of a beloved father. She cherished this legacy as well as another inherited attribute, the ability to spend time happily alone. Both gifts might be needed in her time at Talisman.

The day before she left Meadowmead, Rachel made a round of farewell visits to some of the parishioners who had been particularly fond of the vicar's daughter. They all wished her well and hoped she would be happy in her new place. Ironically, it was only Fanny Dilsworth who seemed glad to see her off.

When the time came at last for her to go, Rachel, however, had conflicting feelings, an inevitable sadness at leaving the gray stone parsonage where she had lived most of her life, mixed with anticipation.

By the time she was on the train headed for Craigburne, Rachel's natural optimism emerged along with her undeniable adventurous streak. She had never been to Cornwall, never been more than fifty miles from Meadowmead. Her thoughts turned from the past to the future and what awaited her at Talisman.

Three hours, two stops, and one change of train later, Rachel stepped out of her compartment at the Craigburne station. The air was clear, crisp with the slight salty tang of the sea. She was tired but excited and looked around eagerly. But there was no one in sight. The few other passengers who had gotten off here seemed to have disappeared. The station house, a white stucco and timbered building surrounded by neat flowerbeds bright with primroses, looked deserted. Mr. Venable had said someone would meet her but there was no one.

Soon the train pulled out again leaving Rachel the only one on the platform. She felt stranded. Had she gotten the wrong day or time? Perhaps they had not received her letter. Maybe she should have sent a telegram.

Then she saw a dignified older man coming along the platform. He was very thin, dressed in a dark coat and striped trousers. His white shirt had a bat-wing collar, dark cravat. Approaching her, he whipped off a black derby hat, revealing a high domed brow and bald head. He bowed slightly.

"Miss Penniston? I am Mr. Venable's butler, Melton."

"Oh, how do you do." Rachel started to put out her hand then realized from his icy look this was neither expected nor proper.

"The Master sends his apologies. He was called away unexpectedly and was unable to come himself to meet you." He raised pale eyebrows. "Is this *all* your luggage?"

"Yes," Rachel replied, feeling she should explain why she didn't have more. "My trunk is being sent."

Melton picked up her suitcase and valise. "The buggy is over there, miss."

Rachel hoped the man's coldness and lugubrious expression were not typical of the rest of the household staff. Carrying her own hatbox containing her best bonnet, she followed him to a shiny black phaeton. The blue-coated driver waited by a gleaming bronze horse's head. The man lifted his top hat as Rachel approached.

"This is Markham, miss." Melton introduced him then assisted Rachel into the buggy. "It's only a short drive to Talisman, miss. It was such a pleasant day Mr. Venable thought you would enjoy the open air."

"How nice. I'm sure I shall," Rachel said, feeling somewhat better that Brett Venable had been so considerate.

After securing her suitcase at the back, Melton got up front in the driver's seat beside Markham, and they started off.

The road from the station went straight through the center of town. The main street was lined with small stores: hardware, bakery, chandlery, fabric, two pubs, a tea shop, greengrocery. A few people standing in doorways and on corners stared curiously as the carriage passed. Having grown up in a village, Rachel knew any stranger stood out and she understood the glances. Perhaps the townfolk recognized the Venable carriage but not the passenger and wondered who she was.

At the end of the main street Rachel noticed a walkway to a long esplanade with wooden benches at intervals overlooking a strip of pebbly beach and a stretch of blue ocean.

They started up a winding hill where at the top stood a large white building whose sign read HARBOR INN. Here, the Venable driver took a sharp turn and they moved onto a country road flanked on one side by a deep wood.

As they turned inland onto a narrower lane, the day seemed to darken slightly. The change was dramatic after the bright spring sunshine. Now low-hanging clouds moved restlessly overhead. A rising wind bent the trees along the way, causing them to sway eerily.

As they traveled farther along the road, Rachel saw the jagged outline of a roof. A bit farther on, a stone fence and wrought iron gates. Passing through them, they started up a winding driveway. To one side, a high, boxwood hedge maze walled the turreted, towered house beyond, like a fortress. In the darkening afternoon, it looked somewhat forbidding.

Pictures came into Rachel's mind of illustrations of castles from some of her childhood storybooks, the kind that used to make her shiver with tales of evil spells, dragons, and imprisoned princesses, of castles that held secrets in their depths, locked away from the outside world. Involuntarily, she shuddered.

"What nonsense!" Rachel quickly checked her imagination. Surely there was nothing sinister about the Venable home.

As they drew closer, the hovering gray clouds seemed to part, and a pale sun gave a luster to the stones and made the house seem what it was, a beautiful eighteenth-century mansion in a tranquil setting of natural beauty.

A handsome chestnut horse was just being led away from the entrance by a groom. Rachel saw Brett Venable, in riding jacket, holding a crop in one hand. He must have just arrived back home himself. Smiling, he came forward to greet her.

"Welcome to Talisman, Miss Penniston. I trust you had a pleasant journey." He held out his hand to assist her down from the buggy. "I'm sorry not to have met you myself, but something unavoidable came up. There are so many last minute things to see to before I leave." He gestured to the front door. "Please come in. The staff is assembled to meet you, and the children are wild with excitement. This is quite an event for them."

Rachel was glad to see Brett Venable's expression was cheerful, his manner relaxed. The dark look of compressed pain so visible at their first meeting was changed, and when he spoke of the children his whole attitude softened, all anxiety vanished. Under his controlled exterior she imagined Brett Venable was capable of deep emotion. He was certainly a sentimental and affectionate father.

He ushered her into a wide hall paneled in a warm, glowing wood. From the room's center rose a curving, carved staircase. "Of course, you have met Melton, Miss Penniston, and now I must introduce you to Mrs. Coulter, our housekeeper, who keeps us all in estimable order."

The woman he introduced was fiftyish, portly, dressed in a gray bombazine dress, its collar lace-trimmed and fastened with an onyx brooch. A ruffled cap nestled in her silver hair. She inclined her head, acknowledged the introduction, and said formally, "Good afternoon, Miss Penniston."

Then, as was her prerogative, she introduced the staff. "This is Gladys, who is the upstairs maid and who will be seeing to your needs. She was the late Mrs. Venable's lady's maid and then became the children's nanny."

A sturdy, robust, young woman, neatly dressed in black with a starched ruffled cap and apron, stepped forward. She eyed Rachel coolly with berry-blue eyes, smiled tightly. There was something about her that puzzled Rachel, as if Gladys had taken an instant dislike to her. Why?

"And this is Molly, the parlor maid." A pretty girl bobbed a curtsey.

"Next is Flora, the downstairs maid." A plain young woman with a nice smile said, "Pleased, I'm sure, miss," for which she got an elbow poke from Gladys that evidently only Rachel saw. Mrs. Coulter went on to introduce Mrs. Bliss, the cook, and Allan, the footman, a good-looking young man.

"There is also the head groom and driver, Markham, who brought you from the station, the gardener, Peterson, the children's riding instructor, Rourke, and stable boys you'll meet later on."

Mrs. Coulter motioned Gladys forward. "Now Gladys will take you up to the combination nursery and schoolroom to meet the children."

Mrs. Coulter stepped back, her duty done, folded her hands at her ample waist from which hung the chatelaine containing a ring of keys, the badge of her authority in the household.

Rachel decided Mrs. Coulter would have to be won slowly to friendship. She was obviously a woman very much aware of the importance and dignity of her position, its power and prestige. She had been cordial but reserved, as if she required time to know a person before extending more than politeness.

Gladys gave a nearly imperceptible toss of her head and without looking directly at Rachel walked briskly to the foot of the staircase. Rachel was about to follow when Mr. Venable spoke.

"I'll come along. I haven't seen the children since I left earlier."

Rachel was glad he was accompanying her, for she wanted her first meeting with the children to go well. Gladys's attitude made her uncomfortable and, with Gladys watching her, Rachel might feel awkward.

Together they mounted the broad staircase in Gladys's wake. Mr. Venable made pleasant conversation and asked Rachel about her trip. As they reached the top of the steps, they heard the sound of voices and laughter before Gladys opened a door at the end of the long upstairs hall.

When they walked into the spacious, cheerful schoolroom, the two children looked startled. The little girl clapped her hand over her mouth to stem the giggles they had heard. The chunky boy, with tawny, tousled hair and dressed in a starched sailor suit, planted himself, hands in his pockets, feet apart, in the middle of the floor. Mr. Venable turned to Rachel, smiling. "Here they are, Miss Penniston, Delphine and Derrick, better known as Dede and Ricky. Come, children, see who I've brought to meet you. Miss Rachel Penniston, your new governess. Come, say hello."

Both hesitated. The boy cast a questioning glance at Gladys. The girl smiled shyly. Rachel felt she should make the first move.

"Hello! I've been looking forward to meeting you both! What a wonderful room. We should have lots of fun together here."

Delphine, an angelic looking child, with waist-length, blond hair that fell in luxuriant waves, moved over to her father and took his hand. She looked up at Rachel with soulful, dark eyes. Slowly, a smile made her small face cherubic, and she said softly, "I'm glad you've come."

Rachel smiled back at her. "I'm glad I came, too."

"Want to see my train set?" challenged Ricky.

Mr. Venable looked at Rachel encouragingly.

"Yes, I'd like that." She moved over to the long, low table on which an elaborate track, station house, tunnel, and a set of miniature train cars was placed.

"I guess you don't need me, sir," Gladys said, startling Rachel by her belligerent tone.

Mr. Venable didn't seem to notice it. "That's quite all right, Gladys. You go right ahead. I'll stay here with Miss Penniston and the children for awhile."

"They have their tea at four," Gladys reminded him sharply before she flounced out of the room.

The next half hour was pleasantly spent. The first awkwardness broken, Rachel was immediately taken by the children. She found them disarmingly unspoiled. They were bright and well mannered, the affection between them and their father touching to watch. As they vied with each other to show Rachel their toys, games, and books, to talk about their ponies, their father seemed totally delighted with them.

Even in so short a time, Rachel came to some conclusions about her future charges. At nine, Delphine had a protective attitude toward her little brother. Perhaps mothering him. Derrick was talkative, aggressive, inclined to be pushy, monopolizing Rachel's attention.

Delphine had just asked Rachel to come see her dollhouse when the door opened and Gladys bustled in with a tray. Rattling china and silver, she conspicuously and noisily went about setting the table for the children's tea.

Mr. Venable gave Rachel an amused look. "I think we're being given a hint," he said to her in a low voice, then he turned to the children. "Well, now, we must be going, and you two must have your tea." He stood up. Both children protested, Derrick clamoring loudly.

"But I wanted to take her—" he pointed at Rachel, "—out to the stables to see my Ginger and Dede's Candy. She *must* see the ponies, Papa!"

His father put up a restraining hand. "Tomorrow will be time enough. Miss Penniston has had a long trip. She needs to have her tea and a little rest, get settled. She'll be here a long time. There'll be plenty of time for the ponies."

Gladys, arms folded, mouth in a straight line, waited stiffly by the table as Rachel said good-bye to the children, promising to see them first thing in the morning. Then she and Mr. Venable went into the hallway.

"I hope all that wasn't too much for you."

"Not at all," she assured him. "They're lovely children."

"I think so, of course. But perhaps I should have allowed you to go to your room, freshen up or rest before throwing you in the lion's den!" He laughed.

"I wanted to meet the children first thing. I think it worked out for the best."

"I'm very pleased. They seemed to like you." He smiled.

Again Rachel thought how changed he looked when he lighted up with a smile or laughter.

Pausing outside a door down the hall, he said, "This is your suite, Miss Penniston. Close to the children's wing, yet far enough so you can have your privacy. I hope everything is satisfactory. If not, let Mrs. Coulter know. And Gladys, of course." He started to leave. "Oh, we dine at seven-thirty. Unfashionably early, I'm afraid. But this is the country. I warned you."

Rachel opened the door and entered the rooms that were to be hers for the next year. She looked around delightedly, walking through the sitting room into the adjoining bedroom. It was as pleasant a place as anyone could wish. In contrast to the austere exterior of Talisman, these rooms were as flowery, feminine, and colorful as she would have chosen for herself had she the means. Cabbage roses in muted colors of pink, mauve, and pale green blossomed on the curtains, bedspread, and plump chairs. It was very luxurious indeed for a young woman who had lived in a shabby vicarage and in cell-like rooms at Havelock Hall as a pupil and later as a teacher.

Perhaps it had been more than good luck to overcome her first reluctance about taking this job in an isolated country house. Perhaps this would be a year of pleasant surprises.

Although Rachel had no way of knowing, there were many surprises ahead for her in this year, and not all of them would be pleasant.

3

*T*hat evening Rachel dined alone with Mr. Venable in a huge dining room handsomely decorated with seventeenth-century mahogany furniture and framed hunting scenes on the wall. The polished table, large enough to seat twenty, dwarfed their two place settings. Candles glowing in tall silver candelabra and a fire burning in the fireplace made it all warmer, less intimidating. Brett Venable's affable manner toward her, more that of an acquaintance than an employer, soon put Rachel at ease.

Elegantly served by Melton, assisted by the footman, Allan, the meal itself was simple; a light mushroom soup was followed by baked chicken, fresh peas, and tiny carrots. With quiet pride Mr. Venable informed Rachel the vegetables came from his own kitchen garden. Horticulture was one of his hobbies of which he talked animatedly during dinner. It was evident from the way he spoke of his gardens and orchards, his interest in herbs, their many uses both medicinal and culinary, that Talisman was very important to him. It would be hard for him to leave his home, especially his children. They, of course, were his favorite subject.

Over dessert, an apricot *creme,* he again expressed his concerns about being away from them so long. Rachel was about to reassure him of her intention to be dedicated in her role when unexpectedly he confided some uncertainty about his sister-in-law.

"She isn't used to the country or children," he said thoughtfully, stirring his coffee. "I suppose I worry because of the things my wife told me about her. I don't know Verdonia well myself. This may seem strange, Miss Penniston, but I have met my sister-in-law only once, and that was at our wedding twelve years ago. She was fifteen years older than Sophia. After Sophia's mother died, Verdonia became a substitute mother for Sophia. She practically raised her. At their father's death, Verdonia took over the management of the family's varied business holdings, and she sent Sophia away to England to boarding school. That is where I met her. She was a friend of my cousin, also a pupil at the school."

He paused, a smile softening his mouth, as if he were thinking of that happy period of his life. Then he sighed deeply. "The management of their father's affairs was quite a responsibility for a woman. Sophia felt it was too much. She knew Verdonia and was afraid carrying such a burden might result in a breakdown. My wife often begged Verdonia to come for a long visit, especially after we came to Talisman and the children were born. But Verdonia always had some excuse—the press of business, she couldn't get away." Again he paused, shook his head. "It seemed strange to me, because Sophia insisted over and over how close they were as sisters, that Verdonia didn't find time to come. Sadly, as it turned out, she never came, and then it was too late."

There was an infinite sadness in Brett Venable's expression. "Sophia became ill and died before we could even get word to Verdonia of how serious the illness was."

Rachel murmured something she hoped was appropriately sympathetic.

"Verdonia was unable to come to the funeral, and though we have corresponded regularly, I have not seen her again in all these years. I'm not sure I'd know her if I saw her." He gave a short laugh. "I had hoped to discuss with her in person some of the matters I have to deal with in Australia, but it cannot be helped. It's a pity, once more our meeting will be postponed. I cannot change my sailing date again."

He shrugged. "I plan to leave detailed questions about the family's Canadian holdings to which I need answers to transact my negotiations there. Verdonia can inform me of her concerns, send me directives through my lawyers or our London bank, or write to me directly where I'll be staying.

"Well, enough about business," Mr. Venable broke off. "I apologize for boring you with such things, Miss Penniston. I'd much rather talk about the children. I'm glad you seem to have won them easily. They need someone other than myself in their lives. Nurses and nannies are very well in their limited roles, but children need more. Don't you agree?"

"I do indeed, Mr. Venable. The children are charming. I feel we will get along splendidly."

"Do you have family, Miss Penniston?"

"Unfortunately not. I always longed for a sister or brother."

"You *did* tell me you were an only child. I have a half-brother, much younger than I. Our growing-up years were separated. Although we do not have a history of the closeness Sophia felt existed between her and Verdonia, after our marriage my brother often spent school vacations with us. He adored Sophia, and she treated him as if he were her own brother."

For a minute or so Mr. Venable seemed lost in some pleasant memory. Then as if newly aware of Rachel's presence, he said almost apologetically, "I should not have burdened you with all this personal family history; however, I did want to ask you to be particularly aware that Verdonia may have some emotional reaction from coming here now, her beloved sister dead, the children poignant reminders of all she has missed. Regret over the past can be devastating. It is a lesson to all of us to live each day to its fullest, appreciate our lives, enjoy the happiness that is ours for whatever brief periods we may have together."

Rachel was moved by Mr. Venable's sincerity and vulnerability.

"I assure you I will make every effort to help Miss Templeton feel comfortable and enjoy the children and the beautiful country."

"Yes, and remember she is used to being busy, constantly concerned with running the business. She may find the isolation depressing, feel somewhat lost or discontented in this environment. I would appreciate it if you would do all you can to help her be happily occupied."

"I will certainly do my best, Mr. Venable."

Mr. Venable stood up. "I'm sure you will, Miss Penniston."

Rachel pushed back her chair and rose from the table. Together they left the dining room and went into the wide hallway. At the staircase Mr. Venable bade her good night. Rachel climbed the stairs slowly. At the landing, she turned to see him going into the room she had been told was the library. In that moment, he seemed a heart-rendingly lonely figure.

4

The next day Mrs. Coulter took Rachel on a tour of the house, Delphine trailing along with them. The mansion was filled with valuable antique furniture, ornately framed paintings, priceless porcelain vases. There were Turkish rugs, exquisite silk Chinese screens, and Italian sculptures in niches. Rachel stopped to admire a pair of twin ebony statues on a table in the upper hall, twelve-inch figures of Moors, turbaned in gold, holding twisted candle sconces.

"Mr. Venable is a great collector," Mrs. Coulter said. "He traveled widely before his marriage, and afterward he and Mrs. Venable went together until the children were born. Then she preferred to stay home with them." Mrs. Coulter's eyes misted. "She was a very devoted mother. Of course, he has tried to make up for her being gone."

She glanced at Delphine, who had moved a little ahead of them and was standing gazing into a glass-fronted cabinet containing etched glass figurines. The child turned to Rachel. "This is my Mama's Lalique collection." She pointed with one small finger. "They're made in France. They were her favorite things. Sometimes she let me take them out and play with them, if I was very careful." She sighed. "And I was. I never broke one!"

Rachel smiled at her. Because of her own motherless childhood Rachel felt a tenderness for the little girl who evidently loved and missed *her* mother very much. Leaning forward Rachel looked into the display of tiny figures. "They're exquisite. I can see why you love them."

Delphine's face lighted up, and she slipped her hand into Rachel's. "You can call me Dede, if you like," she whispered shyly.

Rachel's heart was touched with sweet surprise. She had hoped to gain the friendship of the children gradually. She had not expected to win it this quickly. Dede had accepted her, though Rachel had a strong feeling it might take longer for Ricky. That little fellow had quite an opposite personality from that of his sister.

Just then Brett Venable appeared.

"Getting the grand tour, I see?" he asked approvingly.

Delphine dropped Rachel's hand and ran to her father.

"Yes, Papa! Miss Rachel thinks Mama's Lalique collection is exquisite. She said so." Dede looked back at Rachel. "Didn't you?"

"Yes, I did, and it is!" Rachel met Mr. Venable's gratified look. "It's good when fine things are appreciated."

Delphine swung on his hand. "Can we take Miss Rachel down to see our ponies now, Papa?"

"Capital idea. That is, if she wants to go." He glanced questioningly at Rachel, who nodded. "Where's your brother?"

"He's with Gladys. She's making him do sums. He was naughty and stuck out his tongue at her," she said in a low voice.

"Aha! Well, we'll overlook that for now. Go fetch him. Tell him we're going out to the stables."

"But what about his sums?"

"Too pretty a day for arithmetic." He winked at Rachel. "Besides, it isn't Gladys's job to teach Ricky sums. Not any more. He has a governess now. I suspect Miss Penniston will have her own way of teaching when the time comes."

Delphine went racing down the hall to rescue her brother. Two minutes later, Ricky came running out. He was followed almost immediately by a flushed and furious Gladys. When she saw Mr. Venable she halted.

"I'm letting the children play hooky, Gladys," he told her offhandedly. Then taking both children by the hand, he started down the stairs. "Come along, Miss Penniston."

As Rachel started to follow the trio, she caught Gladys's scathing glance. Those bright blue eyes glittered with animosity. Rachel started to say something, but the maid wheeled around and marched past her down the hall, brushing by Mrs. Coulter as she did.

"Wait, Gladys," Mrs. Coulter said and hurried after her. "Now, Gladys, you mustn't—"

Rachel didn't hear anything more because at the same time from halfway down the stairs both children called, "Miss Rachel, come on!"

With a last look back down the hall, where the housekeeper and maid continued their heated conversation, Rachel went down the steps. Even though she didn't know what was being said, she felt *she* was the subject under discussion. In less than twenty-four hours, she had somehow made at least one enemy at Talisman.

That week before his departure, Brett Venable spent much of his time with the children and with Rachel also. He included her in their excursions and activities. She understood his purpose in doing so. He was showing the children by his example of respect and friendliness how he wanted them to regard her. Rachel realized this was not the usual way a governess was treated. She could not help wonder if the staff at Talisman might misunderstand and possibly resent it. Favoritism always created problems.

The pecking order in this kind of household was always rigid with the butler and housekeeper at the top, the other servants in well-defined places beneath them. In most houses, a governess's position was ambiguous, considered not a servant, yet not a member of the family.

Rachel finally told herself it was not her concern. Brett Venable had hired her. If including her was the way he wanted to insure a solid relationship between her and the children before he left, she would cooperate. Besides, she found his company most agreeable. He was considerate, gracious, and intelligent. She enjoyed the time she spent with him enormously.

Brett Venable and Rachel shared an interest in botany, something Rachel's father had passed on to her when she was growing up. Rachel and Brett had many lively discussions as he showed her the plants he was experimenting with in the greenhouse as well as the herb gardens.

Gladys continued showing hostility toward Rachel, and this troubled her. The times she had tried to engage the maid in conversation had failed. Even a pleasant good morning or a simple question was rebuffed or given an exaggerated "Couldn't say, *miss*" or some equally abrupt reply. Rachel concluded that Gladys was jealous. Until Rachel came, Gladys had been in charge of the children. She had been their mother's maid, then their baby nurse and nanny. She probably felt replaced and rejected, and resented it bitterly.

Rachel knew she would miss Brett Venable more than was proper. She was losing a friend more than an employer. Once he was gone she would have no one with whom she could have interesting discussions on varied subjects. He was always courteous and considerate toward her, with the children, gentle and devoted.

However, in some ways he was an enigma. On several occasions Rachel had noticed a sudden change come over him. Sometimes they would be talking and he would break off mid-sentence, as though losing his train of thought. An unfathomable look of sadness—or was it anger?—would come over him suddenly. At such times he would excuse himself and quickly walk away, his shoulders hunched, hands clenched into fists. Consumed by some deep pain, some hidden secret?

At those times, moved by pity, Rachel felt an urge to reach out, touch his arm, and ask if there were anything she could do. But, of course, she never did. It would be unthinkable. He was the master of a magnificent estate, she the governess to his children, an uncrossable chasm rarely bridged in class-conscious nineteenth-century England.

Perhaps it was the remembered agony of the loss of his beloved wife or the thought he would soon have to part with his children that brought on these strange moods. Whatever it was, Rachel knew she could do nothing to prevent them, nor anything to assuage them.

Two weeks after Rachel's arrival at Talisman, the inevitable day of Brett Venable's departure came. The morning he was to leave he came to her sitting room. She was sorry to see this brief enjoyable interlude with a charming, intelligent gentleman end. She sensed in him a real reluctance to leave his beloved home and children. His voice was husky with emotion as he said good-bye.

"I trust you with my most precious possessions."

"I know," she replied, adding impulsively, "I won't fail you."

Afterward, Rachel hoped her spontaneous words had not sounded overly dramatic. She had spoken from the heart, and she felt Brett Venable understood.

At first, the children were visibly affected by their father's leaving. Rachel made special efforts to distract them from their sadness, however, and within a week they seemed to settle down in their new routine.

The children gradually accepted Rachel as part of their life. Delphine was much easier to manage than Derrick, who tended to be stubborn and willful at times. But with a mixture of firmness and kindness, Rachel won—at least most of the time. She used her storytelling ability, her imagination, and her inventiveness to make lessons fun, playtime instructive. She created a nice balance between the school-

room and outdoor activities. Twice a week their riding instructor came, and Rachel supervised their riding lessons
on their ponies.

With the first week of June, summer arrived with sunny
mornings and long, lovely afternoons. Rachel planned happy
rewards for diligence during lessons such as picnics taken
down to the sheltered cove at the end of the property. There
the children played on the crescent-shaped beach and
waded in the water made shallow by a long sandbar. There
was also a netted court at the side of the house where they
played quoits or badminton, a level stretch of lawn near the
terrace for croquet. One of the children's favorite games was
hide-and-seek in the winding and complex pattern of the
boxwood hedge maze.

Rachel did not push a friendship with Mrs. Coulter. Her
first impression of the lady had been correct. For the first
weeks Rachel was at Talisman, the housekeeper was polite
but reserved in all their encounters. Rachel tactfully consulted her before making any plans about outings or activities she had in mind for the children. This petted the older
woman's ego, and through this solicitous respect and defer-
ence, slowly Mrs. Coulter's manner toward Rachel warmed.

Rachel was not so lucky with the other members of the
staff. Melton kept his distance, maintaining a lofty superiority he apparently deemed due his position. To Rachel's disappointment, there seemed no way to win Gladys, whose
barely concealed resentment simmered constantly just
under the surface. Rachel would have liked to be on friendly
terms. She could have used Gladys's advice in dealing with
the children. Particularly Ricky. He tended to pull tantrums
when thwarted from doing something he was set upon
doing. Reasoning was not always of any use. If it happened
when Gladys was present, she offered no help. It was most
often Delphine who intervened and got her little brother to
behave by diversion or distraction.

Rachel knew this behavior was partly due to the absence of his father and partly because he'd been indulged as the youngest. Still, she could have used some suggestions from Gladys, who had cared for the boy since birth. But Gladys offered only a smug attitude when these upsets occurred, as though nothing like them ever happened when *she* was in charge. Rachel despaired of ever gaining her friendship.

Rachel had only minimal contact with the other servants. Allan, the footman, a cheerful young man, was pleasant enough and had a wonderful way with the children.

Although her days were full, sometimes in the evenings Rachel felt lonely and at loose ends. Even at Havelock Hall there had been some camaraderie among the teachers, some social contact. Brett Venable had warned her, and it wasn't that she was sorry she had come to Talisman. It was just that she would have welcomed some adult conversation and company.

To Rachel's surprise, one afternoon Mrs. Coulter invited her to tea in her apartment in the downstairs wing of the house.

The housekeeper's rooms were pleasant but rather cluttered. A curio cabinet filled with knickknacks stood in one corner, and on nearly every table surface were framed photographs of family, friends, and children in households where she had worked.

The tea table was fastidiously appointed, with beautiful hand-painted china—the gift of a grateful former employer, Mrs. Coulter proudly told Rachel—and embroidered linens, *her* handiwork. The tea was fragrant with thin slices of lemon, and there was a lovely cream cake and strawberries. As Mrs. Coulter did the honors, pouring the steaming amber tea into eggshell-thin cups, Rachel mentioned how impressed she was with Mr. Venable's devotion to his children, how reluctant he had seemed to leave them.

"Oh, he is that, all right. Besides being one of the finest gentlemen for whom it has ever been my good fortune to work. I first came here when they had only been married a year. I've never seen a couple more in love. She was beautiful, as you know from her portrait." Mrs. Coulter shook her head sadly. "I've never seen a man so devastated as he was by her death. If it hadn't been for the children—well, I feared for his life."

She paused and sighed. "But for their sake, he pulled himself together. The more I've come to know Mr. Venable, the more I'm convinced of his sterling character, his real goodness. You would never know he has a *title.*"

"A title?" Rachel took the cup Mrs. Coulter handed her. "You mean he's a lord or—"

"Yes, but you'd never know it. I mean, since he came into it he's the same as he was before. He is the eldest son of a wealthy industrialist, brought up in the best traditions of the landed gentry. His uncle, who was knighted for some service to the monarchy, died recently, unmarried and without an heir. Mr. Venable inherited the title, the fortune, and the vast holdings. *This* house, however, I understand the Venables bought when they got married. It means a great deal to him, and he has refused to move to the estate he inherited."

"All this is surprising. Mr. Venable seems quite without affectation and seems to enjoy the life of a typical country squire."

"He wasn't keen about it all, I can tell you," Mrs. Coulter confided. "He's a man of simple tastes, but there was no one else. A great deal of responsibility and attention is involved, and he is not one to shirk his duties. It takes him away from home and the children more than he likes."

Mrs. Coulter refilled Rachel's cup. "Of course, Master Derrick will inherit it all one day."

So Brett Venable was a *lord of the realm.* In a way, what Mrs. Coulter had related depressed Rachel. Any wild notions about a possible future relationship with her employer were dashed before they had really formed. It was just that Brett Venable had so many of the qualities Rachel had fantasized in her dream lover. He was cultured, intelligent, handsome, charming. How ironic. He was forever out of her reach. Had they met in different circumstances, on more equal ground . . .

*A*s the days passed, Rachel became more comfortable in her new role and fonder of the children. Delphine was easy to love, Derrick a real challenge, more active than his sister, self-absorbed, and stubborn. Perhaps he was too young to remember or miss his mother. Delphine delighted in telling Rachel about her. One afternoon, while Ricky was taking a nap, Dede asked Mrs. Coulter for the key to the glass-fronted cabinet to show Rachel her mother's Lalique collection.

The little girl removed each crystal figurine one by one, holding up each so the light set all its facets sparkling. "Sometimes Mama let me play with them on the floor of her boudoir as a very special treat. They are very delicate, so of course I was very careful. I have to ask for the key from Mrs. Coulter now. But Papa told her I could have it if I promised to open the cabinet only when Ricky wasn't around. It makes me feel—well, close to Mama, somehow." She sighed. "See the little angel? That is one of my favorites. The bird, too."

Rachel was touched by the little girl's willingness to share something that meant so much to her. Dede had a depth of understanding and maturity exceeding her nine years.

Sometimes Rachel noticed Gladys hovering in the background, supposedly putting away linen or doing some other chore. Rachel was sure she was observing, watching her with the children. In a way, it made Rachel self-conscious. In another way, she hoped it would soften Gladys's attitude toward her to see how much she cared for the children and wanted what was best for them. But jealousy was a terrible thing. Once rooted it was hard to displace. Rachel could only pray Gladys would come around in time.

Rachel had been at Talisman nearly four weeks, when late one afternoon, coming up from a picnic at the cove, she and the children saw a man standing on the terrace. He was waving to them with both arms. He looked so familiar, Rachel was startled.

At first she wondered if her eyes were deceiving her. The man looked like Brett Venable. She halted, wondering if for some reason he had returned. Then suddenly both Ricky and Dede broke away from her and ran toward the man shouting, "Uncle Tony, Uncle Tony!"

Rachel hurried after them. Coming closer, she saw clearly it was not Brett Venable, though someone very like him.

When she got to the foot of the terrace, she stopped. The children were clambering all over him, clinging to his jacket. Ricky was exploring his pockets. In turn, he was hugging the children. Over their heads, he glanced up at Rachel, giving her a frankly admiring look.

"Hello there! I'm Townsend Venable, Brett's brother, better known as Uncle Tony. And *you* are Miss Penniston, I'm told. Gladys said these little rascals were off somewhere with their new governess. I'm happy to meet you."

Rachel felt a bit overwhelmed by his ease of manner and confident charm. All she could manage was, "How do you do." Which sounded, even to her, stiff and *governessy*.

The children's voices rose excitedly, preventing any further adult exchange. Rachel was grateful. It gave her a few minutes to collect herself and study the surprise visitor.

Although perhaps a good ten years difference in age separated Brett and his brother, there was a strong family resemblance. The younger Venable was a few inches taller, slimmer of build, his hair a golden brown, inclined to curl. His features were of the same attractive mold. It was in expression where the difference in the brothers was most noticeable. Townsend's mouth was less stern, turning up at the corners, as if always ready to smile. The lips were beautifully shaped, firm yet sensitive.

Rachel wondered how it would feel to be kissed by him. This sudden, irrelevant thought flashed into her mind at the same moment she became aware of Townsend Venable's deep blue eyes regarding her with some amusement. Almost as though he had read her mind.

Blushing furiously, Rachel leaned down to brush non-existent sand from the hem of her skirt and to avoid the eyes that seemed, all at once, knowing.

"I should apologize. I'm afraid I gave you quite a turn, Miss Penniston." He raised one eyebrow. "Didn't Brett mention his scalawag of a brother?"

"Yes. But he didn't say you might visit. We had so many other things to discuss before he left." Her explanation sounded lame, and Townsend's twinkling eyes only made it worse.

"I'm sure you did, Miss Penniston," he teased. "Possibly he thought I was still out of the country. I come and go frequently." He laughed. "Popping in unexpectedly. Keeping everyone off balance. Still, I'm surprised he didn't warn you I might be down to check up on you. Report any ill demeanor." He laughed again. "Don't look so frightened! I'm just joking. When you get to know me better, you'll be able to tell."

He turned back to the children. "Shall we all go in for tea? Mrs. Bliss has promised a special one. Because I've been gone so long and she's missed me. In fact, Gladys says she's been pining her heart out for me!"

Ricky and Dede giggled at his tomfoolery, knowing the cook was well past fifty, fat and jolly but hardly the type to be pining over anyone, much less a young handsome man like Townsend Venable. The children swung the hands he held out for them as they pulled him toward the house. He cast a mischievous look over his shoulder at Rachel. "Come along, Miss Penniston."

Obviously the children both adored him. So must the cook, Rachel decided. Their tea that afternoon *was* special. It boasted two kinds of cake, a variety of rock cookies, and gooey plum tarts.

While Dede and Ricky played happily with a set of brightly painted wooden puppets Tony had brought them as presents, Tony—as he now insisted she call him—directed his attention to Rachel. Over the chatter of the children, he explained he was just back from a year in Italy, where he had served as an embassy aide attached to the diplomatic staff of the English ambassador. He told her Brett had written him about his trip to Australia and requested that when Tony returned to England he look in on the household at Talisman.

"Well, it looks as though I have nothing but good things to report. It seems everything is going swimmingly here." Tony gave Rachel a look that was both appraising and approving. "He must have been convinced you were trustworthy. Still, it's quite a responsibility he's handed you, isn't it?"

"Well, yes, but it isn't one I am going to have to shoulder completely alone. His sister-in-law, Miss Templeton, is scheduled to arrive within a few weeks to be in charge of the household along with Mrs. Coulter."

Tony blew a long, low whistle. "*Verdonia?* Verdonia is coming—*here?*"

Rachel felt a small tremor of alarm. "Yes. Why do you seem surprised?"

"Well, I can only guess—I suppose Brett was feeling rather desperate. Verdonia Templeton seems the last person he would call on to come and supervise his home and children while he is on the other side of the world."

For a moment the perpetually cheerful expression on Tony Venable's face became pensive. "I probably shouldn't even comment. I hardly remember her. I was a mere school-boy at the time Brett and Sophia were married. Down from Eton on holiday, actually, and more interested in devouring the delicious food served at the bridal reception, I'm afraid, than the attending relatives." He grinned. "I was, after all, a starving student at the time.

"However, about Verdonia." He paused, rubbing his chin thoughtfully. "I know Sophia wanted her to come—many times before this. There was always some excuse. Sophia once confided she wasn't sure Verdonia liked the English, the country, or little children for that matter. I can't say for sure—except—" Tony laughed heartily, then lowered his voice. "Except she cheated at croquet."

Rachel took a sip of her tea, feeling it wouldn't be quite proper to laugh at Tony's remark. Though a harmless joke, it was a rather derogatory statement about a woman whom she had yet to meet. A woman who would be head of the household at Talisman.

"I do remember Verdonia being entirely different from Sophia," Tony went on. "Sophia was delightful. Brett adored her, and I fancy I had an adolescent crush in spite of the bib-lical injunction on coveting your brother's wife. I was all of fourteen, I think, and Sophia was lovely—an angel, but fun as well. The times I came down here will always be wonder-ful memories for me." He sighed.

"Delphine is very like her in appearance, in personality, too, I believe. She'll grow up to be a beauty. Like Sophia. You've seen her portrait, haven't you? And then there's an album full of photographs of her with the children. Photog-raphy was one of Brett's hobbies and his family was his fa-vorite subject." Tony shook his head sadly. "Such a tragedy.

Poor old fellow. Talk about marriages made in heaven—theirs certainly was."

Just then Gladys tapped at the sitting room door and came in. Ignoring Rachel, she spoke directly to Tony.

"Mrs. Coulter would like to see you, Mr. Townsend, before you leave, if you'd please come up to her room, sir?"

With seeming reluctance Tony got to his feet. "I better go pay my respects. Keep myself in good graces." His eyes twinkled. "Besides, I should be on my way. I'm a guest of the Alvestons at their home a few miles from here. A proper guest should not disappear for hours without explanation. Especially a bachelor. We rely on invitations to brighten our solitary lives, nourish us with excellent meals, and provide the delightful company of the eligible lady friends of our hostesses."

Tony smiled ruefully. "When did you say Verdonia was coming?"

"Mr. Venable said she would let us know when she arrived in London and would be down a few days later. At least, that is what I understand they agreed upon."

"Well, I shall look forward to getting reacquainted with the lady, although I wager *she* remembers me no more than I do her." Tony shrugged, then he said good-bye to the children, who put up a fuss about his leaving until he promised he would come back soon.

Rachel found herself sorry to see Tony go. His coming had been a surprise, a very pleasant one. She had warmed immediately to his outgoing, friendly personality, his lack of affectation, and his infectious sense of humor.

She did find his reaction to Verdonia Templeton's coming curious, however, and she was puzzled why Brett Venable had not mentioned the possibility of his brother's visiting Talisman. From Tony's conversation, he had been a frequent guest here when Sophia was alive. Did Tony remind Brett too poignantly of happier days? Had the brothers drifted apart since Sophia's death? Possibly, as Tony suggested, his brother had not been sure when Tony would return from Italy. It sounded as though his schedule was erratic.

Tony's relationship with the children seemed a natural, joyous one, and he was on great terms with Mrs. Coulter, Mrs. Bliss, Gladys, and the other servants. Curious to know more about the relationship between the brothers, Rachel decided to tactfully question the housekeeper. Mrs. Coulter was a fount of information about Talisman.

Rachel was surprised and delighted when two days later Tony reappeared. He offhandedly explained the house party was dull, his fellow guests uninteresting, and he'd wanted to come back to see the children again before returning to London. Secretly Rachel hoped seeing her again was included in his reason for returning to Talisman.

Since the weather was still balmy and warm, Rachel had planned to take a picnic and spend the day in the little cove where the children could wade and play in the sand. The children begged Tony to come along, but he seemed to need no persuasion. It was a perfect place for the children to float the toy sailboats Tony had brought them.

After they had eaten their picnic of ham sandwiches, lemonade, grapes, and ginger cookies, the children ran down to the water's edge. Rachel and Tony found a sun-warmed dune where they could sit and talk while they watched Dede and Ricky. Tony seemed as eager to know all about Rachel as he was to tell her about himself.

"Actually, Brett and I are half brothers, coincidentally like Sophia and Verdonia, with about the same number of years separating us in age. Brett's mother died shortly after he was born, and our father did not remarry for some ten years. Then to a much younger woman, *my* mother. Brett always treated me with affection, and the fact we had different mothers did not ever seem to enter into our relationship. Of course, due to the age difference, our paths did not cross often. Especially when I finished school. Brett was busy managing his estate, becoming a devoted husband and father, while—" He stopped, gave a little shrug. "I'm afraid I was pursuing an entirely carefree existence. Well, not really. I started reading law but decided it was too sedentary a life for me. I'm restless, you see, crave change, adventure. I took off and for a whole year traveled—on my own—through Europe."

"That must have been exciting! I've never been anywhere. I was brought up in a village and went to school in a small town and now—here I am."

"You'd love some of the places I went, I'm sure. Italy is marvelous. Venice, Florence, Rome! Glorious. That's where I made my decision to see if I could get into some kind of work where travel would be part of it. I've been quite lucky."

"And do you know where you'll go from here?"

Tony shook his head. "I'll be in London for some time, I think. They like to rotate our service, not let anyone become an expatriate. Life in some of these Mediterranean countries can be seductive. So much more relaxed than in England."

Rachel found herself responding more and more to this fascinating young man. Her interested attention led him into telling her more stories of the intriguing people he'd met, the customs he'd encountered, the castles, museums, and historical sites he'd visited. He waxed most enthusiastic about the side trips he'd made on his own, some on foot, some on a donkey, through southern Spain.

"A regular Don Quixote!" she exclaimed, laughing.

"Jousting at windmills?" He looked a little chagrined. "I admit I'm drawn to the unmarked path, the untraveled road, the unexpected encounter. I guess I'm a gypsy at heart."

Rachel felt her own heart leap at his words. Was that what she was, too? Why she felt that secret longing for an open road stretching into the unknown where romance and adventure waited?

The wind off the lagoon rose, sending ripples that rocked the children's tiny boats. Shadows stretched across the sand. Reluctantly, Rachel called to the children. Tony helped pack their picnic things back into the wicker basket, and they all headed back to the house.

Upstairs in the schoolroom, Tony suggested he teach the children an Italian folk song and directed Rachel to the piano to pick out a few simple chords. A hilarious time ensued as the three of them stumbled over the Italian words Tony said slowly. They finally caught on enough to sing loudly, if not accurately, for the next half hour. Tony's rich tenor helped smooth out the slightly off-key voices of the children. Rachel was reduced to helpless laughter and could hardly keep playing. Of course, the children loved it.

When at length Tony said he must go, they pleaded for him to stay. As with his last visit, only his promise he'd be down again as soon as he could satisfied them. Rachel was equally sorry to see him go and chided herself for caring so much.

The children were hard to settle down after Tony left. It had been an exciting day, and it took Gladys's help to get them tucked into bed at last, but by the time Rachel finished the story of the "Six Dancing Princesses," little eyelids had begun to droop.

Later, in her own room, Rachel admitted to herself Tony Venable had made quite an impression. Rachel could not deny she found him immensely attractive. What young woman wouldn't? He was charming, amusing, witty, *and* good-looking! What a hopeless romantic she was. To say nothing of being fickle! Her first fantasies had been about the unattainable Brett Venable.

Besides, didn't she realize his younger brother was also in a higher social echelon, just as unattainable? A romantic relationship with either of the Venables was only for the realm of impossible daydreams. Life wasn't a fairy tale where princes married penniless peasants. Even well-educated ones!

Maybe her father had made a mistake broadening her intellect, giving her *ideas and airs,* as Fanny Dilsworth used to say when she saw Rachel translating a book of German poetry.

What an odd life she had. From a sheltered life in a country vicarage to a rich country estate with her head in the clouds.

For Tony, stationed in London, taking the train down for the weekend was easy, and after his first visit, he became a frequent visitor at Talisman. In spite of her inner cautioning, Rachel looked forward to his coming and regretted seeing him go.

One Sunday evening, after Tony had delayed his leaving until the last possible train back to London, and the children were tucked in at last, Rachel found herself alone in her sitting room, lost in thought. She couldn't remember when she had enjoyed herself as much. Tony Venable had made such a difference in her life at Talisman. What if she hadn't taken this job, never come here, never met him . . . Suddenly, Rachel knew, in spite of everything she had told herself, she had fallen foolishly in love.

Rachel had no time to indulge in "if onlys," nor in useless regrets. Only a few days after that idyllic weekend and the dismay of her self-revelation about Tony, something happened to make her personal concerns secondary. A cablegram was delivered to Talisman. It was from Verdonia Templeton, announcing her sailing date from Canada and her scheduled arrival in Southampton. She would send further information on her plans from there. This sent Mrs. Coulter into a tizzy, ordering a complete housecleaning and turning the staff upside down in preparation for Verdonia's coming.

When Tony came the following weekend, Rachel told him of Verdonia's imminent arrival.

He made a comic face. "I'm afraid you're in for it, Rachel."

"What do you mean?" Rachel felt a stirring of apprehension.

"Oh, just that Verdonia—or the Verdonia I remember—was a take-charge sort of person. I pity Mrs. Coulter. Verdonia will turn the housekeeping arrangements upside down, reorganize everything!"

At Rachel's look of alarm, Tony laughed. "I'm painting a terrible picture for you!"

"Well—" Rachel dragged out the word.

"Don't take me so seriously. I'm no fortune-teller. I just recall a remark Brett once made about her. I'm sure spoken out of frustration. Something about Verdonia being the proverbial spectre at the wedding feast. I guess she wasn't too keen on her precious younger sister marrying. She wanted her to come back to Canada, I suppose. Marry someone there. I don't know. It will all work out."

Rachel devoutly hoped so. But Tony's remarks, albeit spoken in fun, lingered troublingly. Rachel took some comfort in his departing words as he prepared to return to London late Sunday afternoon.

"Don't worry about Verdonia's coming. I'll be the official welcoming committee and apply all the diplomacy and charm I'm supposed to be acquiring in my job. We'll have Miss Verdonia Templeton eating out of our hands. She'll be as sweet and docile and accommodating as the tame deer in the park."

However, as it turned out, midweek Rachel received a dismaying note from him. The hastily scribbled note said, "Due to saber rattling in some obscure Balkan principality, the fate of the Empire evidently hangs by the proverbial thread. I am off on a peace-keeping mission and cannot say when I'll be back on British soil, nor able to enjoy your delightful company again."

Rachel's disappointment was, she told herself, out of all proportion. She shouldn't let it matter so much. She should think of Tony Venable as a friend. Surely nothing more. But all this sensible self scolding did not alter the fact she felt let down and wondered how long it would be before she saw him again.

The following day a telegram arrived at Talisman. Melton brought it to Rachel because Mrs. Coulter was taking her afternoon rest. No one ever disturbed her at that time of the afternoon. At the sight of the yellow envelope, Rachel experienced her instinctive aversion. As Melton handed it to her, she had to curb a shudder.

Under his impassive stare, Rachel quickly composed herself. She knew her feelings were understandable, associated with the personal tragedy a telegram recalled. However, this time her reaction felt different. As she opened the envelope, a strange foreboding came over her. It had nothing to do with the contents. The telegram was from Verdonia Templeton and simply stated she had arrived in Southampton. She would travel to London, stay there a few days to rest and do some shopping. She would let them know the day and time of her train from London.

Calmly, Rachel relayed the information to Melton and asked him to inform the staff. But she could not shake her peculiar reaction to the message. She had the strangest feeling that with the arrival of Verdonia Templeton life at Talisman would change. And not for the better.

6

The children were very excited at the prospect of Aunt Verdonia's arrival.

"She was Mama's older sister," Delphine informed Rachel when told about the telegram. "Very *much* older. Mama was only a little girl when Aunt Verdonia was already a grown-up lady. Mama said Verdonia took care of her when their mother died. She even gave up a beau so she could stay with her and not leave her alone to be raised by nannies."

Rachel listened with interest. Delphine obviously had loved hearing her mother's stories.

Although Ricky had little memory of Sophia except what Delphine told him, he was just as interested in the arrival of his Canadian aunt, eager to participate in the preparations for her coming. Rachel helped the children gather flowers to make into nosegays wrapped in laboriously cut out paper frills. They crayoned greeting cards to place in her room. Mrs. Coulter planned to serve a festive tea when she arrived from the train station.

Rachel wished desperately Tony was going to be here to help welcome Verdonia Templeton. It was foolish, she knew, but despite all the careful preparations, she had the most dreadful feelings of presage.

The day of Verdonia's scheduled arrival, the household was in an uproar. Mrs. Coulter was everywhere at once, supervising the maids as they scurried about doing a final dusting, inspecting every detail. Rachel arranged the loveliest of the garden flowers in cut-glass vases to place in the rooms of the suite Verdonia was to occupy.

When Rachel took up one of the bouquets, she looked around the beautifully appointed rooms overlooking the terrace and maze. Everything was in perfect readiness. Any woman would be delighted with the graceful French furniture upholstered in tufted peach satin, the pastel flowered rugs. An exquisite Chinese screen, framed in teakwood and embroidered in silk, stood between the sitting room and the hall. While Rachel was admiring everything, Gladys, her arms piled with towels, came by.

Surprisingly she opened a conversation. "Fit for a queen, I'd say! I hope her ladyship appreciates all the trouble we've gone to for her." She gave a dismissing sniff. "But knowing Miss Verdonia—"

"Oh, that's right, Gladys. *You* know Miss Templeton, don't you? You're the only one who does, actually."

"Well, I can't say I really know her. I only seen her when she came for Miss Sophia's wedding, and that's been nearly twelve years ago. Before we came to Talisman." Gladys shook her head. "I was Miss Sophia's maid in London before she married Mr. Venable. Miss Sophia had pictures of her sister, but *she* weren't a bit like Miss Sophia, she wasn't. *My* lady was the sweetest lady you can imagine. Smiling, kind to everyone. While Miss Verdonia—"

Gladys shrugged and shifted her armload, opened the armoire and carefully placed the linens and towels on the shelves, arranged the bags of sachet that scented them before closing the doors. "I don't know what it was about her— a kind of look down her nose sort of way she had—"

Whatever more Gladys was about to say was cut off by Mrs. Coulter. Passing by in the hall, she stopped in the doorway. "Gladys, you've got more to do than to be standing around chatting, haven't you?"

"Yes, ma'am. I was just putting away the linens," Gladys replied.

Then the housekeeper noticed Rachel and said sharply, "Shouldn't you be getting ready to go to the train station? Melton will be bringing the barouche around to the front any minute now."

Mrs. Coulter bustled off, the ring of keys at her waist rattling. That wasn't Mrs. Coulter's usual way of addressing her. Rachel felt reproved until she saw Gladys roll her eyes upward and pull a comic face behind the housekeeper's departing figure, which took some of the sting out of the reprimand and, Rachel hoped, indicated a step toward friendship.

Parodying a wince, Rachel hurried to her room to change her outfit for the trip to the train station.

Melton was to check the scheduled arrival time of the train Verdonia Templeton was taking from London. Mrs. Coulter had assigned Rachel the duty of going with Melton to the station. It was *hers* to be on hand to welcome the lady to Talisman.

Rachel dressed with understandable nervousness. This first meeting with the woman who would be in charge of the household for the next eleven months of Mr. Venable's absence was important. The woman would be, in essence, Rachel's employer. First impressions were always crucial, often forming lasting opinions, hard to change.

Her lilac poplin dress was suitable, Rachel decided, and with her straw bonnet trimmed with purple ribbons, it struck the right note of discreet good taste. Just as she was buttoning her gloves, a knock sounded on her bedroom door.

When she opened it, she found a grave Melton standing there, behind him, an ashen Mrs. Coulter, just visible beside her, a wide-eyed Gladys.

"What is it?" Rachel asked, knowing by the expressions on all three faces something dreadful must have happened.

"I'm afraid it's bad news, miss," Melton said. "Quite terrible, actually. News has just come from the village that on its approach into Craigburne, the London train collided with another train on the same track."

"Oh, Rachel, they say it's awful." Mrs. Coulter's voice trembled. "A terrible wreck. Many injured, some dead. They're still pulling people out of the wreckage."

"Miss, that's the train Miss Templeton was scheduled to come on," Gladys volunteered, her voice unnaturally high from the horror and excitement of it all.

"That's true, miss. I'm very much afraid, miss, very much, indeed. If Miss Templeton *was* on that train—" Melton let whatever his fears were go unspoken.

"Rachel, dear, you must go with Melton at once to the station, see what you can find out. I'm much too shaken to accompany you. But someone from Talisman must—" Mrs. Coulter patted her perspiring forehead and upper lip with a dainty, lace-edged hanky.

Rachel steadied herself by leaning on the door frame. An accident. Verdonia Templeton hurt, possibly killed. Mr. Venable thousands of miles away.

"Oh, my! What should we do?" she murmured, not really expecting anyone to tell her. They were all looking to her for instructions. She nodded her head. "Yes, of course, we must go down to the station at once, Melton. That's where there'll be the most information available. They must have a list of passengers, where they are, if taken to the hospital or—" She didn't dare finish the sentence.

Rachel knew enough from reading accounts of railroad tragedies graphically written up in newspapers that it might be a horrible sight. Rows of cars built of steel, glass, and iron as they were, traveling at the speeds they did, smashing into another such vehicle of like metals, could mean only disaster, bodies crushed, broken, mangled. She shuddered, feeling a little sick.

"Yes, miss, that would be best. Then if we have any news of Miss Templeton—" Melton let his thought die on his tongue.

With a quick, "Take care of the children," Rachel grabbed her shawl and started past Mrs. Coulter, who caught and pressed her hand.

"That's a good girl, Rachel. I'll be praying that—"

What or who Mrs. Coulter would pray for were lost to Rachel as she hurried by her and down the stairway, out to where the coachman was waiting with the barouche.

Rachel sat tensely forward on the seat all the way into the village, imagining the worst. Oh, if Tony were only here. Nothing in her life before had prepared Rachel for such a situation. Should she send word at once to Brett Venable? Wait until she found out something definite? If his sister-in-law were badly injured or—heaven forbid—*killed*, he must be notified. And what of the rest of the year at Talisman? What of the folder of business instructions he had left for Miss Templeton, containing "matters a woman of her business acumen will understand and can handle." No one else had that responsibility. Rachel realized she did not even know the name of the business enterprises in Canada of which Verdonia Templeton was the director.

"Sufficient for the day is the evil thereof." The old biblical admonition to trust God just for the day's need came into Rachel's mind, giving her strength for the moment. Which, hands clenched, was all she could ask.

At the train station, all was confusion and chaos. People milling about. Prospective passengers waiting to board the ill-fated train from Craigburne to farther stations on the line. Distraught-looking people probably expecting to meet visitors or family members arriving on the wrecked train. As

Rachel and Melton moved through the crowd, they heard rumors, snatches of news. The overturned train was somewhere up the track, not visible from the train platform except for the plumes of black smoke rising ominously into the sky.

They were told that some of the injured were trapped in the wreckage, that rescue workers were still trying to get them out. The strident clang of bells rang constantly above frantic shouts, raised voices, anguished cries. Rachel tried to make sense of all the scattered bits of information she could gather. The most encouraging word she got was that the injured and dying passengers had been removed from the badly damaged train compartments after receiving emergency care from doctors called to the scene. She learned from one harried railroad employee that some of the most badly injured had already been taken by ambulance or other conveyance to hospitals as far away as London. Eventually a list of names of passengers would be posted so that next of kin could find those missing.

After an hour or more of futile inquiry and searching for some clue to Verdonia Templeton's welfare or whereabouts, Rachel and Melton decided all they could do was return to Talisman and wait until further information about the wreck and its casualties or survivors was given by the authorities.

St. Ambrose Hospice

Before she opened her eyes she was conscious of a pounding headache. When she tried to lift her head a sharp pain knifed through the base of her skull.

She tried to raise herself, but the slightest movement made her flinch. Her whole body felt stiff and bruised. She lay there listening to muted sounds, muffled voices as if from a long distance away. She realized she must be in a hospital. How she knew that, she did not understand, because she had never been in one before. She tried to move but was pinned down by coarse sheets pulled tightly over her. Gradually a vague remembrance of what had happened sifted through the thrumming in her temples.

She remembered that brief moment of panic before the terrifying jolt, the crash of steel, shattering glass. The screams of other passengers had dissolved in a hideous blackness.

The pain in her head, neck, and shoulders stabbed again, and she moaned. Slowly, whatever medication they'd given her sent her drifting off, even as she tried to remember exactly what had happened.

The next thing she knew she was awakened by someone giving her cheeks smart little slaps.

"Hello there! They want you to wake up now."

Two faces leaned above her, one a man's, the other a woman's framed by a stiff, white nurse's veil. She *was* in a hospital. Slowly things began to come through to her fuzzy brain. The train. The accident.

"She's coming round now. Are you in pain?" An expression of concern crossed the man's face. "I'm Dr. Lorimer, and this is Sister Graves. You're at St. Ambrose Hospice. You were in a train wreck."

She stared at him blankly. It was all coming back now. Did they know what had happened just before the impact, the crashing sound of metal, shattering glass?

"Can you tell us your name?" She ran her tongue across dry lips. Of course she knew who she was. But her throat was dry as sand.

Other questions followed in fast succession. "Where do you live? Can you tell us whom we may call to let them know you're all right? Some relative? Family? Friends? Try hard now." The man's voice persisted.

"I can't remember—" She was about to say "exactly what happened," but the doctor didn't let her finish.

He patted her hand reassuringly. "Never mind. Luckily we have your identification. It was in the purse you were clutching when they brought you in. Don't exert yourself. We have your things safely put away. All of it will come back to you in time. You were not seriously injured. You need a little rest, that's all. You'll be right as rain." His voice faded, and she closed her eyes again.

She didn't know for how long she had slept when the door opened again and a tall, ruddy-cheeked man with a thatch of graying hair entered. It was lighter. She could see him better. Was this the same one who'd been here before? He gave her a sharp look.

"Well, you're looking a great deal better this morning. Most of the bruising is fading. Anyway, you ladies have clever ways of dealing with that sort of thing, don't you? At least that's what my wife says. Veils, large brimmed hats. Not to worry, the black and blue will gradually fade, and you'll be as pretty as ever, I dare say."

What a fatuous fool the man was, she thought disdainfully. She'd had her share of men flirt with her, ogle her, but this doctor was someone she would never give a tumble, if it came to that. She closed her eyes again, and when she opened them he'd gone.

They brought her a breakfast tray. She was hungry, and the tea was hot and strengthening. She was nibbling toast when the nurse came back in with clothes on a hanger.

"Good morning," she chirped. "My, but you're looking much improved. I'm Nurse Evans, and here are your things. They've been cleaned and pressed, good as new. I'll be back later and help you dress." The nurse whisked out again.

When she finished eating, she put her tray aside and got out of bed. Examining the outfit the nurse had hung up on the closet door, she didn't recognize anything. There must have been some sort of mix-up. Everything was well made, but frightfully plain, with labels from some of the best London stores. She fingered the material of the traveling suit of fine blue tweed, collared in darker blue velvet, a cream silk blouse with fluted jabot. Not waiting for the nurse to return, she began to dress. Her muscles were still sore and stiff as she moved. She picked up the hat, brushed the feathered crown thoughtfully. Then she turned to the small mirror over the washstand to put it on. Something caused her to lean closer. She pulled out a few strands of hair, examined them, frowning. Gray! She'd have to do something about *that*. She put on the hat, tucking the telltale hair well beneath the brim, then adjusted the veil. She turned this way and that. Not bad. She shrugged. Bit of luck, actually.

Fear stirred in the pit of her stomach. She felt suddenly dizzy, swayed, reached out her hand to steady herself. Nausea threatened, but she gritted her teeth, took a long breath. She'd experienced this sickening feeling before—often—like stage fright. She couldn't let on though, or they'd keep her here longer and maybe . . .

Nurse Evans breezed in and seeing her clutching the bedpost, pale and swaying slightly, exclaimed, "Be careful now, Miss Templeton. You're apt to feel somewhat dizzy and not quite yourself yet. But soon everything will right itself, and you'll be just fine. Once you're in a familiar place, among familiar faces, you'll do just fine. Like the doctor said, you're one of the lucky ones. Lucky you were clutching your handbag when they brought you in. That's how we found your identification and were able to notify the people at Talisman." Noticing the woman was looking in the mirror at the bonnet with some distaste the nurse said quickly, "That one was found in the train compartment they pulled you out of and we just assumed it was yours. You've got more than enough money to buy a new hat if you like." Nurse Evans set down a small overnight case with the initials VT on the clasp. "Here's the valise that was also in your compartment. It has enough in it so you'll do fine until they locate the rest of your luggage. I still say you're lucky."

Yes, she thought, the nurse was right. She always had been lucky somehow. In spite of everything, she'd always managed to land on her feet. Just like a cat.

She turned around quickly, gathered up the soft leather handbag containing her train ticket stub that indicated her destination as Craigburne. Unsure just where that would lead, she straightened her shoulders, lifted her chin defiantly, and walked through the door the nurse held open for her.

*A*pprised by the hospital that Verdonia was on her way and would arrive by the afternoon train, Rachel's nerves jangled. The letter from the hospital's attending physician had briefly outlined Verdonia's injuries. "Minor but may have lingering effect. Due to the concussion her speech may seem halting, she may seem vague, or have frequent periods of memory loss or irritability. These symptoms are not considered serious. Otherwise Miss Templeton appears to be in good health, and all these above-mentioned symptoms should disappear given proper rest, quiet, and freedom from stress."

Having already been warned by Brett Venable that his sister-in-law's health was fragile, Rachel felt some trepidation. The take-charge person Tony had described was now a semi-invalid. What new responsibilities this would place upon *her*, Rachel had no idea. It was understandable Verdonia had suffered severe shock. Still the prospect of dealing with a traumatized victim of such an accident was daunting.

The entire household was in a flurry of preparation. Rachel went along with Mrs. Coulter for a last-minute check of the suite Verdonia was to occupy. The housekeeper nervously circled the room, smoothing the bedspread, sliding her hand down the folds of the draperies where they fell into silken pools on the flowered carpet, touching the tasseled drapery cords. Her eyes darted about anxiously. In an attempt to reassure her, Rachel said, "Everything looks perfect, Mrs. Coulter. It's a beautiful room, a lovely place for someone to recuperate from such a horrible experience as Miss Templeton has had."

"Yes, yes, I think so," the housekeeper murmured. "It's just that I do want her to feel comfortable here."

"I'm sure she will, Mrs. Coulter."

Satisfied at last, the two ladies went out to the hallway where they parted. Mrs. Coulter hurried downstairs to confer with the cook on the special tea to be served when Verdonia arrived, and Rachel went to get ready to accompany Melton to the train station.

Before she left, Rachel cautioned the children not to be too loud or exuberant in their welcome. "Remember, your aunt has spent weeks in the hospital, and the doctors say she's still far from strong. We need to give her plenty of quiet to recover."

Both little faces fell but brightened again as Rachel promised them a special treat if they would be good and do as they were asked. Then she pulled on her gloves, tightened her bonnet ribbons, and went out to where Melton waited with the enclosed carriage. Even though it was summer and the weather mild, Mrs. Coulter suggested it might not be beneficial for one so recently up from a sickbed to ride in the open air.

Rachel hoped she would have no trouble recognizing Verdonia Templeton when she got off the train. She had already formed a mental picture of her, paler and thinner than she might have looked had she arrived promptly after a sea voyage from Canada. Again, Rachel wished Tony were not out of the country. After all he *had* met Verdonia Templeton, even if that was years ago.

Rachel had little actual description of Miss Templeton. The one photograph she had seen was of the bridal party at the Venables' wedding. Unfortunately, at the moment the camera snapped, the bride's sister had evidently moved and her image was blurred. That picture was hardly enough to go on to recognize someone twelve years later. Did the sisters bear a family likeness as Tony and Brett did? In the wedding photograph, Sophia appeared to be blond, although the veil she wore covered most of her hair. The slanted brim of the wide Gainsborough her bridesmaid, Verdonia, was wearing concealed much of her face. Rachel decided she would just have to trust her intuition when the train arrived.

As it turned out, very few passengers got off the train that afternoon. Rachel scanned each one. Then she saw a tall, elegantly dressed woman step out of a first-class compartment and stand on the platform looking about rather dazedly. She looked about the right age and as though she were expecting to be met. Rachel hurried toward her.

"Miss Templeton? I'm Rachel Penniston. The Venable children's governess. I've come to take you home to Talisman."

The woman did not reply at once. The veil on her hat shadowed her eyes and the rest of her face. She was obviously still in shock, confused. Trying to put her more at ease, Rachel said, "I understand you've been through a great deal, but it is only a short ride through very pleasant countryside. As soon as we get there, you can rest. Please come with me."

"My things," Verdonia murmured, making a vague gesture with her hand.

"The hospital said most of the luggage was being held by the railroad company and will be delivered for owner identification. I'm sure it will come soon. Now, you aren't to worry about anything."

Still the woman seemed to hesitate. She seemed indecisive and unfocused. The doctors had warned of this. Rachel just needed to be soothing and reassuring. She shouldn't expect Miss Templeton to behave normally after what she had been through.

Rachel tried to be warm without being overwhelming. It was a puzzling situation. She would have to be tactful. She gently took Verdonia's arm and led her to where Melton stood waiting by the Venable carriage. He opened the door for them, then joined the coachman on the driver's seat.

As they started off, Rachel tried to make pleasant conversation, telling Verdonia how eagerly the children were waiting to greet her, how concerned they had all been about her injuries in the train wreck.

Verdonia said something in so low a voice Rachel could barely hear her. She neither offered comment nor initiated any other conversation, just stared steadily out the window. Sitting stiffly, as far away from Rachel and to her own side of the carriage as she could, her arms crossed, hugging her body as if she were cold, she made little reply to any of Rachel's further attempts at conversation. Through her veil, when she turned to stare at Rachel, her expression was blank, eyes glazed.

Rachel finally gave up. After all, the doctors had warned that the effects of a concussion could be lingering. Verdonia *had* a concussion. People often took a long time to completely recover. She reminded herself Verdonia should not be expected to carry on a social conversation or be pressured in any way. Simply allowed to rest and relax.

As they drove along in silence, Rachel studied the other woman. Her profile was quite lovely, even though the chin line was softening, natural in a woman over forty. The mouth, although now pursed as if in pain, was full, sensuously curved. Kid-gloved hands were clasped tensely upon the alligator handbag she held in her lap. Verdonia seemed strung as tightly as a wire. Nerves, Rachel concluded. She had been through a great deal.

Mrs. Coulter had suggested they have the Venable family doctor on hand to check Verdonia upon her arrival so he would be acquainted with her condition should the need arise to call him once she was settled at Talisman. It would be more for their own peace of mind to know that a physician was available in case there were complications.

As they neared the house, Rachel saw Dr. Holden's buggy in front and explained his presence to Verdonia. This seemed to agitate her.

"I've had enough of doctors!" she exclaimed indignantly in a voice that surprised Rachel with its deep, husky tone. "I just need to be left alone!"

Taken aback, Rachel explained as calmly as possible why this had seemed necessary in view that there might be effects of her injuries that had not shown up immediately but might later do so.

Verdonia hunched her shoulders, tossed her head, did not answer.

Mrs. Coulter, all anxious fluster, was waiting at the front door alongside Dr. Holden when the carriage came to a stop in front of the house. Solicitously, she came out to help Verdonia alight, but Verdonia shook off the plump hand reaching out to her. Dr. Holden, his ruddy-cheeked face framed by bushy, mutton-chop sideburns, stepped forward and introduced himself. He was given almost as short shrift as Mrs. Coulter had received.

Trying to reclaim his dignity, he blustered, "We just want to be sure, my dear lady, that the very traumatic event you underwent does not cause you any further problems. I shall be pleased to come at once to administer any kind of—"

"I'm all right, thank you. All I need is some peace and quiet." Verdonia spoke firmly. "Now, if someone will just show me where I can lie down, I'm very tired from my trip from London."

She did not even seem to see the two children, little bouquets of flowers clutched in their hands, waiting hopefully on either side of Gladys just a little bit behind Dr. Holden. Immediately Mrs. Coulter bustled ahead, and taking her cue, Rachel followed a few steps behind Verdonia as they went upstairs to the room prepared for her.

At the landing, Rachel looked back and saw Dr. Holden standing, mouth open, looking after them. The good doctor, well-liked and respected in Craigburne, had probably never before received such disdainful dismissal.

At the door of the suite long awaiting her, Verdonia made no comment. She flatly turned down Mrs. Coulter's timid suggestion she send one of the maids up to help her undress and get into bed.

"I don't need that. I'll make my own decisions," she said firmly. "I would like some tea and something to eat. Perhaps some sherry, too. Medicinal, so the hospital staff tells me."

"Of course, Miss Templeton. Right away."

Rachel and Mrs. Coulter left the room. In the hall outside the closed door, they exchanged a single glance. Rachel knew, as well as Mrs. Coulter, it was totally beyond their place to discuss a member of the family who employed them. Rachel remembered Brett Venable telling her he and Sophia had found Verdonia hard to understand. Perhaps a natural standoffishness, coupled with the trauma of the accident, had made her even more difficult.

Downstairs, Mrs. Coulter tried to mollify Dr. Holden, who had somewhat recovered from the treatment from his would-be patient.

"Don't trouble yourself about it on my account, dear madam. It is understandable given what the lady has been through. Just give her time. I advise plenty of rest and calm. Given her history, Mrs. Coulter, I would simply try not to upset her in any way until she is fully recovered."

As he started out the front door with his unopened medical bag, he turned and said, "In case she should have trouble sleeping—nightmares, sleeplessness are sometimes an effect of a serious accident—I would be happy to prescribe some laudanum."

"Thank you, Dr. Holden. I'll pass that on to Miss Templeton. I'm sure she'll be grateful." Mrs. Coulter followed the doctor outside, embarrassed she had brought the busy physician out such a long way on a proverbial wild goose chase, to say nothing of his having endured a rather unpleasant encounter with an ungrateful lady. "Thank you so much for coming," she called after him as he climbed into his buggy. When Mrs. Coulter came back into the hall, her mouth was pursed, her face quite flushed. Rachel could see the whole incident had upset the housekeeper and boded ill for her relationship with the new mistress of Talisman.

Rachel had to comfort the children in their disappointment of not being able to put on the welcome they had planned for their aunt. Rachel took them for a romp. They played a riotous game of hide-and-seek in the maze, far enough away from the house so their laughter and voices wouldn't reach the open window of the second-floor room where Verdonia now lay in solitary luxury.

Later Rachel thought over the events of the afternoon. Her first impression of Verdonia Templeton was shaded by the things she had heard about her beforehand. But her initial meeting had not changed the generally negative opinion voiced by both Tony and Gladys. Usually Rachel tried to avoid making snap judgments. However, Verdonia Templeton's arrival at Talisman had somehow reinforced the strange uneasiness she had felt about her coming.

8

hree days passed. The house seemed on tiptoe, held in thrall by the strange behavior of their recently arrived guest, who remained secluded in her rooms. Rachel longed to talk to someone about the strange situation, one she felt sure was being openly discussed in the servants' hall. Certainly Gladys, assigned as Miss Templeton's maid, would have an opinion. Rachel could often tell by her expression that she didn't enjoy being at the newcomer's beck and call, lugging heavy copper vats of hot water up the stairs for her bath, carrying trays with pots of tea up to her at all hours.

No one else caught a glimpse of Miss Templeton except Mrs. Coulter. The housekeeper paid a daily visit on the lady and came away with a puzzled frown on her usually placid face. If she happened to pass Rachel in the hall or on the stairway she averted her eyes, obviously suppressing comment. Both Rachel and the housekeeper knew it was not proper to indulge in talk about an employer.

At first the children complained because they hadn't met their auntie, but then they seemed to lose interest and went about their daily lives as if she had never come.

Rachel felt her first responsibility was to take care of the children, and given the circumstances, to keep them away from Verdonia's wing of the house as much as possible, lest their childish high spirits, bursts of laughter, or running up and down the halls or on the stairs might disturb their ailing aunt.

The evident strain Mrs. Coulter was under resulted in one of her periodic migraines, and on the fourth morning she sent for Rachel. In her darkened bedroom, she turned over the task of her daily call on Verdonia. Mrs. Coulter was in agony, so Rachel could only accept the assignment with good grace.

She met Gladys in the hall as the maid was bringing out Miss Templeton's breakfast tray. Rachel asked her if she would take the children out to the garden while she visited Miss Templeton.

"No need to speak so softly, Miss Penniston." Gladys jerked her head toward Verdonia's closed door. "The *duchess* seems to have completely recovered!"

Rachel's glance followed the maid's departing back. There was no mistaking the cutting edge of her remark. It did not take Rachel long to find out for herself its validity. She tapped lightly at the door, waited until the voice called out, "Come!"

Entering, Rachel saw a quite different Verdonia Templeton than the dazed, disoriented woman she had first met.

Verdonia was lying on the chaise lounge near the open French windows. She seemed to have come out of her benumbed condition and looked peevish and petulant.

"Good morning, Miss Templeton," Rachel greeted her. "Mrs. Coulter is a little under the weather today, and she asked if I would look in on you and see if there was anything you needed or wanted."

Verdonia frowned, studied Rachel for a full minute, as if trying to place her. "And you are?"

"Rachel. Rachel Penniston, the children's governess." Had Miss Templeton forgotten it was *she* who had met her at the train? Was the head injury more serious than they had been told?

"Of course. It just slipped my mind for a minute." Verdonia passed a hand over her forehead, shook back the masses of auburn hair that hung loosely to her shoulders. "Being in these strange surroundings with all these strangers, it's hard for me to get a grip on reality. The doctors said it might be like that."

"Yes, we all understand, Miss Templeton, and we want to make you as comfortable as possible. Is there anything special we could get you or do for you?"

Verdonia gathered the negligee about her, then swung her legs over the edge of the chaise. As she did so, satin folds fell back, revealing a length of shapely leg. She leaned forward to thrust her feet into marabou trimmed slippers, and Rachel was faced with the top of her head. Were the roots dark compared to the shiny brilliance of the rest of her hair? It seemed incongruous that Verdonia Templeton, whom she'd been told was of a rigid, almost prudish nature, dyed her hair.

"I'd like the London papers for one thing. And some wine with my meals. Medicinal, you understand. The doctors recommended it would be helpful in regaining my strength and improving my appetite." Her voice sounded irritated, dissatisfied. It certainly held the demanding tone of a duchess.

"Yes, of course, Miss Templeton. I'll relay your request to Melton. He is in charge of the wine cellar. We'll send an order to the village bookseller to have the London papers delivered daily."

Verdonia walked over to the dressing table. Her carriage was erect and her movements graceful. She picked up a silver-backed brush and comb, regarded herself in the mirror with a slight frown, then returned to the chaise.

"Good. And some novels. French ones, preferably."

"The weather is quite lovely still, Miss Templeton. Mrs. Coulter suggested you might enjoy sitting on the terrace in the sunshine. We could easily move a reclining chair out there for you."

"Maybe," Verdonia replied indifferently. "I'll see." She picked up a few of the small satin, lace-edged pillows, then sat down again, tucked them behind her neck and leaned back.

Rachel stood there a minute longer, wondering if she should wait to be dismissed. Verdonia looked so bored she decided to risk another suggestion. "The children are very anxious to see you, Miss Templeton. I wondered if I might bring them in for a short visit later in the afternoon, just to say hello?"

"I think not." Verdonia looked pained. "I'm not quite up to *that*. I need a few more days rest before—children can be quite tiring, as well as tiresome."

"I believe you will find your niece and nephew to be exceptionally well-behaved, lovable children." Rachel realized her tone was slightly defensive.

Verdonia shot a quick, appraising look at Rachel, then as if to soften the remark, flashed a smile that made her almost beautiful. "Oh, I'm sure they are. It's just I'm not as strong as I thought I was. But do give the little dears my love. I'm looking forward to being with them. *Soon.*"

Rachel left Verdonia's suite feeling confused. In the space of less than fifteen minutes she had received a number of conflicting impressions.

Other than the carriage ride from the train station, this had been Rachel's first opportunity to study Verdonia Templeton. She was far different than either the blurred photograph or the mental picture Rachel had of her. The day she arrived, her face had been hidden by a concealing veil. Today Rachel had the chance to really see it. There were definite traces of earlier youthful beauty. Faint lines between her eyebrows and around her mouth were the only telltale evidence of aging. If she were sixteen years older than her sister, Sophia, who had died at age thirty-one, Verdonia Templeton was well into her forties.

It was, however, an arresting face, mobile, capable of shifting shades of expression. During their brief conversation it shifted swiftly from petulance to animation to moodiness to amiability.

Verdonia Templeton seemed as enveloped in mystery as she had seemed when Rachel had known only her name.

A little more than a week later Verdonia sent a message through Gladys to Rachel that she wanted the children brought to her after her bath for a mid-morning tea party. Surprised, Rachel got them ready. She brushed Delphine's hair until it shone with lights and tied her sash. Getting Ricky into a crisp, white sailor suit and fussing until his navy blue silk tie was just right was another matter. Wiggling and squirming, he demanded, "Can we ask her about the train wreck?"

"I don't know whether she wants to talk about that," Rachel replied doubtfully as she slicked down his unruly mop of curls. "It was an awful thing to happen."

"It *was* exciting though, wasn't it, Rachel?" Dede persisted. "I mean getting rescued and all like Aunt Verdonia was, and being taken to hospital and being in a—a— what was it?"

"A coma."

"What's a coma?" Ricky screwed up his face in puzzlement.

"It's when you go to sleep from a hit on the head and don't wake up for days," Dede explained.

"I wouldn't like *that!*"

"Well, it isn't exactly like that. She had what the doctors call a concussion. It's a really bad headache and sometimes—well, never mind." Rachel decided it was too complicated to try to explain to a pair of seven- and nine-year-old children. She'd take them in to see their aunt, and they could draw their own conclusions as to her condition.

"Now, remember, we're not to stay long, nor to tire her," Rachel whispered outside Verdonia's door.

Rachel need not have worried. Looking rested, almost radiant, Verdonia welcomed the children with enthusiasm and a great show of affection. The visit turned out to be a complete success. To Rachel's astonishment, Verdonia was charming and warm with the children, who were at first shy then gradually became their naturally winning selves.

The children, thrilled by the dramatic way Verdonia had entered their lives, were ready to accept her as an object both of glamour and drama. What became a daily courtesy visit to their aunt lengthened until they spent a good part of each afternoon hovering about Verdonia. They were on their best behavior around her.

"They're like little drones around the Queen Bee, ain't they?" Gladys commented waspishly. Rachel was inclined to agree. The children seemed enchanted by their languid, mysterious auntie who had come from so far and had such an adventure. They became her willing little courtiers, ready to do her every bidding, fulfill her least whim. Verdonia seemed amused by their obvious adoration and urged Rachel to leave them alone with her. "I'm enjoying getting acquainted with my niece and nephew. I feel I've missed a great deal not being with them."

This left Rachel with hours on her own even though she insisted on their lessons being done before their going to Verdonia's suite. She found that during their lesson time, the children were distracted. Dede's eyes were often on the schoolroom clock more than on her schoolbooks.

Rachel had to admit to a slight twinge of jealousy. She felt somewhat excluded from the afternoons they spent with Verdonia. The children's keen interest in Verdonia and hers in them did not escape Gladys's notice. Nor her commenting on it.

One day Rachel was straightening bookshelves in the schoolroom when Gladys came in to clean the adjoining bedroom. As she stripped the beds and piled the sheets into the laundry basket, she cast several glances in Rachel's direction.

Finally she came to the doorway and without preamble asked, "What do you think of Miss Delphine and Master Derrick spending so much time with Miss Verdonia?" Without waiting for Rachel to reply, Gladys went on. "Seems kinda strange for a grown woman, 'specially one *supposedly* recovering from such a bad shock, you might say, to want to have two lively young children scrambling around her for hours at a time, don't it to you?

"I was doing her bedroom the other day, and I couldn't help hearing wot they was all talking about." Crossing her arms on her plump bosom, Gladys put her head to one side. "She asks them all sorts of questions about their father, wants to read his letters to them. Now, I find that kinda odd."

The implication required some answer, but Rachel hesitated. To discuss the children's aunt with a servant wasn't wise. Yet this was the second time Gladys had shown an inclination to be friendly, and Rachel did not want to cut it off. Besides she knew Gladys loved the children, wanted only the best for them.

"Maybe it's because she hasn't been here in so long—twelve years, didn't you tell me? That and with the accident, her concussion and all, she may have forgotten things and wants to refresh her memory."

"Hmmph," was Gladys's only response. She made quick work finishing the bedroom and went off, obviously miffed.

Rachel reminded herself that gossip with servants was never a good idea. However, she mulled over Gladys's comments. Her own contacts with Miss Templeton had been few and superficial, usually in the presence of the children, yet Rachel found herself curiously fascinated by Verdonia. Maybe it was because she was from Canada that she seemed different. Her manner was often abrupt, even abrasive. Or this could be because, as Mr. Venable had told Rachel, Verdonia was a businesswoman. She was used to making decisions, giving orders, expecting them to be obeyed. At times she was quite gracious. Still, there was something elusive about her that puzzled Rachel. Then she remembered Brett

Venable's statement that his sister-in-law was—what had he said?—difficult.

If the children were charmed by their glamorous aunt, Mrs. Coulter was not. In charge of the servants' daily routine, the housekeeper resented the constant demands the woman made of the servants. Requests for snacks and special food at irregular times kept Mrs. Coulter in a constant frenzy. The maintaining of an orderly schedule was continually interrupted. Flora had to be sent into the village on an errand, or hot water had to be heated in the middle of the day because Verdonia wanted to wash her hair. Verdonia's complaints were vocal and plentiful. The smallest thing could send her into a display of temper. Bath water too hot, tea not hot enough, or one of the London papers not delivered on time. Her outbursts were over quickly, as soon as they were appeased, but they were upsetting to a household used to running smoothly. The current of discontent ran high, frazzling Mrs. Coulter's nerves. Her tension spilled over onto the rest of the staff, who became testy, short with each other, generally touchy, like a bunch of snapping turtles.

As a result Rachel often went to bed emotionally weary but unable to sleep. She often read late into the night in the hope it would make her sleepy enough. Sometimes she awakened stiff and aching from falling asleep in a twisted position, a book open on her lap, her oil lamp sputtering.

One night Rachel awoke abruptly but didn't know why. She lay tense, straining to hear whatever it was that had awakened her. She heard what sounded like footsteps moving stealthily along the hallway outside her room. Who could be up prowling around at this time of the night? One of the children? Rachel reached for her wrap and got out of bed. She slid into her slippers and crossed the room, opened the door into the hall.

It was dark, of course. She would have to get her lamp to see anything. Just as she turned around, she heard the sound of a door clicking shut at the other end of the corridor. Verdonia's wing. Her door?

Rachel halted; could those footsteps have been Verdonia's? Was she sleepwalking? That was one of several symptoms Dr. Holden had said could be the result of a severe blow to the head. Rachel stood quite still. She heard nothing else. Not a sound. Could it have been her imagination?

She hurried back into her room, over to the bedside table, picked up her oil lamp, turned up the wick, struck a match and lighted it. Then she went back into the hall and made her way along the corridor to the children's bedroom. Both of them were sleeping soundly. Neither stirred when she smoothed their hair and tucked in their blankets.

Rachel returned to the hallway and went back to her own bedroom. Still she felt uneasy. If what she had heard was Verdonia, was this a new aberration stemming from her concussion? If so, should she report it to Dr. Holden? Sleepwalking could be dangerous. Rachel had read of people falling off balconies or down staircases.

Perhaps she should go see Dr. Holden, get some professional advice. First, though, she should discuss it with Mrs. Coulter.

$\mathcal{T}$alking to Mrs. Coulter about her new worries of Verdonia's possible sleepwalking was out of the question the next day. Mrs. Coulter was in no condition to discuss anything, much less anything to do with Verdonia Templeton. She sent word she had another sick headache and Rachel would have to deal with the cook and make all other arrangements for the day.

With the housekeeper's duties imposed upon her, Rachel went to the kitchen to go over the day's menu with Mrs. Bliss. The cook was uncharacteristically glum and made plaintive remarks about not being appreciated.

When Rachel questioned her, Mrs. Bliss's eyes reddened, and she sighed heavily. "Never since I had my first position as cook have I ever had one of my puddings sent back, as *lumpy,* mind you. And everyone's always told me my lemon sauce was the best ever."

"And it *is,* Mrs. Bliss."

Mrs. Bliss's lower lip trembled. "Well, *evidently,* Miss Templeton don't think so."

Rachel spent half an hour trying to reassure the cook before she seemed mollified.

No wonder Mrs. Coulter gets migraines, Rachel thought as she hurried out to the front of the house to make sure Flora and the girl who came from the village to help were busy at their chores. They were whispering as she walked into the drawing room. Dust lay thick on the furniture. At her entrance, they started dusting frantically, so Rachel left. She had her own job of supervising the children's lessons still to do without taking on scolding housemaids.

Rachel was so busy for the rest of the day her strange experience of the night before was pushed to the back of her mind.

When late that afternoon Tony Venable arrived, Rachel was inordinately happy to see him.

"I didn't expect you! When did you get back?" She tried not to show her delight. However, she couldn't control the warmth rising into her cheeks when she saw the lovely bouquet he held.

"I should have sent word, I guess. I've only been back a few days. I guess I'm so used to popping down here whenever I have a chance, I didn't think. Mrs. Coulter never seemed to mind, and certainly Brett and the children didn't—" He paused and gave her a mischievous look. "Do *you?*"

"Not at all," she said, feeling flustered. "It's just that Mrs. Coulter is not feeling well, and Miss Templeton—"

"That's really why I've come. To pay my respects. I thought it high time I put in an appearance to welcome her. These are for her." He handed the flowers to Rachel. "Will you give these to the lady and present me? I doubt if she'll remember me but—"

Hiding her disappointment that the bouquet was not for her, Rachel said quickly, "I suppose you don't know?"

"Know what?"

"About the accident. The train wreck?"

"I've been out of the country, Rachel. I have no idea what you're talking about."

Rachel filled him in on the details of the train wreck and Verdonia's hospitalization.

"Good heavens! Does Brett know? How badly was she hurt?"

"Thankfully, not seriously. The doctors said a concussion, some bruises mainly. But—well, there have been some—the doctors said there might be—some vagueness, some forgetfulness—natural results of a blow to the head."

Tony frowned. "Well, thank God for that. A letter from my brother just caught up with me, forwarded from the embassy to my London flat. He asked Verdonia to come to England while he was gone, not so much for the children, but because of her experience. He was depending on her to handle some of the business affairs connected to the joint estate—investments, quarterly payments, that sort of thing. Out of Mrs. Coulter's realm, certainly, and definitely not your responsibility. But she should be able to do that in time, I imagine. She is recovering, right? No complications?"

"Just the ones I mentioned. But you can see for yourself. Having known her before, you might be the best judge of whether she is back to normal."

"It's been years." Tony shook his head. "But, yes, I'd like to see her."

"She's kept mostly to her suite, saying she's not up to dressing or coming downstairs. But surely she'll want to see *you*. I'll take these up and say you're here. Would you like to wait in the drawing room?"

"No, I'll just dash up and see the children."

"The children are with *her.*"

Tony's eyebrows arched. "I thought she was recovering from her injuries. Two lively little rogues don't tire her?"

"She seems to enjoy them."

"Verdonia?" He sounded surprised.

Rachel hesitated. "I think I better tell her you're here and want to see her before . . ."

Tony shrugged. "I'll leave that to you."

Rachel heard the murmur of voices behind Verdonia's door and tapped lightly.

Verdonia was on her chaise, the two children standing on either side of her, looking at a large, leather photograph album. When Rachel entered, Delphine looked up, saying happily, "I'm showing Aunt Verdonia our family album, pictures of Mama and us!"

"I'm sorry to interrupt, but Mr. Venable's brother is here, Miss Templeton, and wishes to see you."

Verdonia's expression altered immediately. "Oh, no, I couldn't possibly see him. See anyone. I'm just not up to it." She passed the back of her hand across her forehead in an oddly theatrical gesture.

"He's come all the way from London," Rachel ventured, thinking the least Verdonia could do was say hello to her brother-in-law's younger brother after all these years.

"You *heard* me! I don't want to see anyone—I can't!"

The children seemed startled by the sharp tone of her voice and turned to gaze at her. Dede and Ricky glanced quickly at Rachel then back at Verdonia, eyes wide.

"But it's *Uncle Tony*," Ricky protested, scrambling up from the floor.

"I don't care *who* it is! I won't see anyone." With an impatient movement, Verdonia slammed the photo album closed. "That's it! And take the children with you. I'm feeling quite weary."

"Very well. Come, children."

Subdued, the children ran over to where Rachel stood at the door. Dede slipped her hand into Rachel's, and Ricky tugged at her skirt.

"Draw the blinds before you go," Verdonia ordered as Rachel turned to leave.

Rachel did what she was bid and left with the children, closing the door quietly behind her. Ricky broke away immediately and ran down the stairway.

Dede looked up at Rachel. "Why was Aunt Verdonia so cross?"

"She still isn't well, dear. We have to be patient," was all Rachel could manage. She was both irritated and puzzled herself about Verdonia's erratic behavior.

"I was showing her Mama's album with all the pictures of the trips she and Papa used to take. Pictures of Ricky and me when we were babies. She seemed to be having a good time before you came to tell her Uncle Tony was here."

"It's all right. Sometimes people who have been ill have sudden changes of mood. We just have to accept them. Soon your aunt will be all well." Rachel wished she herself was as convinced as she tried to sound.

Whatever the reaction both children had to the incident in Verdonia's room, they thoroughly enjoyed Tony's visit. He was his usual good-natured self, full of jokes and stories.

The children wanted to go down to the cove. Tony agreed but said first he must make his usual visit to the kitchen, to talk and tease the cook, to chat with Melton.

He was gone a good fifteen minutes before returning to join the children and Rachel, who were waiting for him in the garden. As Dede and Ricky ran ahead, he and Rachel had a chance to talk.

"So how are *you* doing?" he asked as they started down the path leading to the cove. "I gather the invalid is sometimes a trifle difficult."

Rachel hesitated. He had probably gotten an earful behind the baize door. Still, she debated answering Tony's question honestly, telling him the whole truth of just how difficult Miss Templeton *really* was. On the other hand, she was tempted to confide in him, ask his advice.

Her hesitation caused him to stop short and give her a quizzical look. "What is it? Is something wrong? Something I should know about?"

Rachel felt caught in the middle.

In Brett Venable's absence, his sister-in-law was temporary mistress at Talisman. The thing that disturbed Rachel most was the arrogant way Verdonia treated the household staff, including Mrs. Coulter. Rachel was well aware a housekeeper held a special position in the homes of the gentry, always treated with great respect. Servants were also dealt with kindly by ladies of quality. Rachel had often seen Gladys angrily leave Verdonia's room. Even in Rachel's presence, Verdonia had shown little consideration for any of the servants. But how could Tony help with any of that? And if she told him, it would sound like repeating servants' complaints.

"It's probably not important. I mean, when she's feeling better maybe—"

Tony touched Rachel's arm. "If it's bothering you, I think you should say. Is it something Brett should know about?"

Rachel hadn't thought about that. She looked with some alarm at Tony, who was regarding her seriously.

"I don't think so. I guess we're all going through a period of adjustment. Miss Templeton's coming—well, it has rather upset the staff."

Tony frowned, then still holding Rachel by the arm, he continued walking beside her.

"I guess that's natural enough. A person—especially one who has to be catered to somewhat—moving in and being in a position of authority simply by her relationship . . . I'd try not to worry too much. After all, it's Mrs. Coulter's job to keep things running smoothly. Not yours. You've enough to do with looking after the children."

"That's just it—" Impulsively Rachel started to tell Tony she worried about them spending so much time with Verdonia, becoming as Gladys sarcastically put it "right little slaves" to her every whim. She would have tried to explain why that worried her as much as anything else. However, there wasn't a chance.

Ricky came running up and grabbed Tony's hand, imploring him to come down to the water to help sail the toy boat he had brought along.

"All right, young fellow. Let's go." With a rueful smile, Tony let himself be drawn down to the sandy bank, leaving Rachel to follow. She wondered if she should have said anything at all to Tony about Verdonia.

She reminded herself of what Tony had said. She *was* only the governess. He had not meant it in any disparaging way; however, it had the result of reminding *her* of the wide difference in their social stations.

The rest of the afternoon was spent happily enough playing with the children, having tea on the terrace, where Tony amused them all with stories about some of the events and people he had encountered during his recent trip abroad. At length, Gladys appeared to take the children upstairs for their baths. Even when Tony promised he would be down soon again, they left reluctantly.

Secretly Rachel was just as sorry to see him go. She walked with him around the house to wait for the footman to come around with the small buggy to take him to the village to catch the late afternoon train back to London.

"I'll make it a point to come down soon. Perhaps next weekend if I can manage it. Can Mrs. Coulter put me up, do you think, without upsetting the household too much?" he asked, half-teasing, half-serious.

Rachel smiled, feeling unreasonably happy. "I'm sure she will be glad to. You're quite the favorite at Talisman with the staff."

Tony took her hand and gently drew her into the shadowed portico. "And am I a favorite with you, too, Rachel?"

Rachel started in happy surprise. Although *she* had thought of him as Tony, it was the first time he had ever used her first name. The social protocol of names was extremely important. For a man to use a lady's first name was significant. It was the first step to further intimacy, one rarely taken except to indicate romantic interest.

Before she could think of anything to say in reply, Tony leaned forward, those clear, truth-seeking eyes close, his mouth—the one she had thought might be nice to kiss— only inches from hers.

Rachel drew in her breath, but just then heard the crunch of wheels, the clop of horses' hooves on the stone drive.

Tony stepped back. "Good-bye, Rachel. *Arrivederci!* That's Italian for *until we meet again.*" He was still smiling as he gave her a small salute and sprang up into the buggy.

Rachel's heart was pounding, her knees weak, as she mounted the stairway to go up to see to the children's supper and story reading before bedtime.

Just as she reached the top of the steps and was heading to the children's wing, she heard her name called. Surprised she turned to see Verdonia standing at the door to her suite in her nightgown and flowing wrapper.

"Miss Penniston, come here for a minute. I want to speak to you."

It was a command. Stifling a feeling of resentment Rachel walked toward her.

_F_ollowing Verdonia into her sitting room, Rachel was startled at its general disarray. A knitted shawl was thrown across the chaise. On the table beside it were strewn a half-empty glass of wine, a book, facedown, an open box of candy, discarded wrappers. Newspapers had been tossed on the floor.

Verdonia walked to the center of the room, then giving the train of her robe a kick, whirled around and asked, "Did Mr. Venable's brother stay all afternoon?"

"Yes."

"I thought so. I heard voices and laughter on the terrace. It's right under my bedroom, you know, and it woke me from my nap."

Rachel felt guilty, as she was sure was Verdonia's intention. "I'm sorry, I didn't think. We could have had our tea elsewhere."

"It doesn't matter. I just didn't know who or what was making all the noise. I looked out the window—he's very handsome, isn't he?" A smile briefly touched her lips. "I'd forgotten . . . I haven't seen him for a long time."

"He's very like Mr. Venable," Rachel said.

"Yes, I suppose he is. Of course, I haven't seen either of them for quite awhile. Is he coming down again soon?"

"Possibly next weekend," Rachel replied, feeling unreasonably—*what?*

"Be sure and let me know when he comes again. It's time I get out and about, enjoy some adult company."

A few days later when a note came to Rachel saying Tony would not be down to Talisman the coming weekend, her disappointment was keen. He wrote he had to go with a group from the embassy accompanying one of the diplomats on a trip to France. He promised to let Rachel know when he returned to England and could next visit Talisman. At the end he had written, "I long to see you again." That scribbled phrase set her head spinning, her heart leaping with hope. Perhaps, after all. . . . Anything was possible.

Still, Rachel chided herself for feeling so let down he wasn't coming. As dangerous as being around Tony was to her good sense, to be without him was worse.

Life went on as usual at Talisman, or as usual as it had been since the arrival of Verdonia Templeton. Verdonia visibly gained strength, but she still required her meals brought up on a tray. She became increasingly demanding, ringing her bell for service regardless of how busy the servants were at their other duties.

Her attitude toward the children also changed, much to Rachel's dismay. Where at first she had courted the children, now she tired of them easily, seemed bored with their companionship. Her behavior with them was unpredictable, sometimes agreeable, even fawning, other times irritable and sharp.

Summer was at its peak with long sunny days, lovely long twilights. At Verdonia's request, a lounge was placed on the terrace for her to enjoy the balmy air and sunshine.

One afternoon Dede and Ricky were outside with her. Rachel remained in her sitting room reading. A chance to get to the new Trollope novel, she told herself. The truth was, Rachel felt, or more correctly was *made* to feel, superfluous when the children were with their aunt. However, she had left her door ajar in case either child needed her. She had only been reading a short time when there was a rap. She looked up to see Gladys.

"Pardon me, miss, but if you've got a spare minute, I'd like to speak to you about Miss Verdonia and the children."

Rachel slipped a finger into her book to mark her place. "Of course, Gladys. What is it?"

Gladys stepped into the room and closed the door. She seemed positively bristling with indignation. "Well, miss, I dunno wot exactly we can do about it, it's jest that I hate to see Dede hurt." Gladys's bright blue eyes flashed angrily.

"What do you mean?" Rachel was at once alert. Anything concerning the children concerned *her* as well. She knew Gladys felt the same way. Something must be very much amiss. "Whatever it is, Gladys, I'll do what I can."

"It's jest what I seen, miss, sometimes when I'm in there, in *her* rooms straightening up or dustin' and they take a *lot* of straightening and pickin' up, I'll tell you, the way she throws things about, clothes and newspapers and teacups and glasses and—"

Realizing *this* litany of complaints could go on indefinitely, Rachel interrupted. "Yes, Gladys, but what about the children?"

"Well, miss, when the children's in there with *her,* she plays favorites, she does, and teases real mean like. I seen little Delphine get tears in her eyes at some of the things Miss Templeton says to her. Miss Templeton makes Ricky laugh *at* his sister. I think it's a terrible shame, miss, I do. Those two used to play together like nice friends, they did, afore this. Not that they wouldn't get into a scrap or squabble a time or two, but on the whole, miss, they were the sweetest brother and sister I ever did see. Now, well, it jest ain't right."

Rachel felt her own indignation rise. Dismay and frustration followed. "I don't know what I can do about it, Gladys. After all, Miss Templeton *is* their aunt. . . ." Rachel's voice trailed off.

What Gladys had told her had upset her just as much as Gladys. The difference was that as a servant Gladys felt helpless. She'd come to Rachel, depending on *her* to take some action. And she *would*. She had to. After all the children were *her* responsibility.

Mr. Venable had emphasized that over and over. He'd entrusted her to take care of them, to protect them, even from their aunt, if necessary. She remembered him saying Verdonia was not used to children. To give her the benefit of the doubt, maybe she simply didn't know how to deal with children, didn't realize how sensitive little ones could be, how easily wounded by a careless word, a thoughtless jest.

"You did right to tell me. I'll pay more attention to what's going on. I'll speak to Miss Templeton myself."

That seemed to satisfy Gladys. She went out of the room looking more or less satisfied, though leaving Rachel the worse for the conversation. Rachel wasn't sure just how to approach Verdonia on such a delicate issue.

During the next few days, Rachel made it a point to observe the children when they were with Verdonia. She made excuses to bring in the London papers when they were delivered, bring up the morning snack or tea tray. Without Verdonia being aware she was being watched, Rachel saw several incidents that confirmed what Gladys had reported.

One, in particular, moved Rachel to intervene. Verdonia was brushing Delphine's hair rather roughly. Rachel saw the little girl grimace a couple of times when the brush caught a tangle. Instead of working the tangled strand gently through with her fingers, Verdonia yanked and brought tears to the child's eyes, a little cry of "ouch!" Certainly a normal response from any child, but Verdonia gave the little girl's head a smack with the back of the silver-backed brush, exclaiming, "What a crybaby! Look at your sister, Ricky, isn't she a crybaby!"

Delphine's face turned crimson, and tears spilled down her cheeks.

Verdonia gave her a push. "Go away, baby. I don't like crybabies."

Incensed, Rachel crossed the room. Almost too angry to speak, she took Delphine's moist hand in hers. "It's time for your piano lesson. Come along with me."

She didn't dare address herself to Verdonia, afraid she would lash out, vent her anger. As they were leaving the room, Rachel heard Verdonia saying to Ricky, "Come over here, sweetheart, have a bonbon. Sweets to the sweet, and you are such a pet!"

By the time she and Delphine reached the children's wing, Rachel was breathing hard. She wiped the child's flushed face, smoothed back her hair gently. Looking into the small humiliated face, she asked, "Would you like to go into the village with me for a little treat?"

Delphine nodded.

After that day's incident, Rachel planned things for Delphine to do apart from the other two. The little girl seemed more than happy to walk to the village with Rachel on invented errands, to help Rachel wind yarn or cut flowers in the garden. However, Rachel saw she missed her little brother and often felt lonely and left out. Verdonia, for her part, had made no secret she preferred Ricky because he was entirely content to be her little errand boy, fed with chocolates, pampered and petted for her own purposes.

In the midst of Rachel's increasing worries about the situation Verdonia had created with the children, Tony appeared unannounced. At the first sight of him, Rachel forgot her decision to be cool and distant, her instant happiness mixed with relief. Perhaps his presence could defuse the tension rampant at Talisman.

"No time to let you know!" he told Rachel and a flustered but still welcoming Mrs. Coulter. "I just got back day before yesterday and have only today off. I have to go back to London this evening, but I couldn't wait to see you all again." His gaze rested on Rachel significantly.

"You'll stay to tea, surely, Mr. Townsend?" Mrs. Coulter asked.

"Most assuredly, Mrs. Coulter. I've been dreaming of Mrs. Bliss's cherry tarts. Tell her French cuisine is vastly overrated!"

Chuckling, the housekeeper bustled off at once to inform the cook of their unexpected guest, leaving Tony and Rachel alone.

"So, how are things proceeding with the reclusive houseguest?" he asked her. It was only then that her burst of happiness at his arrival deflated. She remembered Verdonia's request, or rather her demand.

"Miss Templeton is well enough to receive you. In fact, she made a point of asking me to be sure to let her know the next time you came. If you'll excuse me, I'll go up and tell her you're here."

"Wait, Rachel," Tony said, taking hold of her hand as she started away, swinging her back to him. "Aren't you going to give me a proper welcome, say you missed me and you're glad I'm back?"

His eyes sparkled and his mouth—the one she had dreamed of kissing—was lifted in a smile that made her silly heart flutter.

"Why do I have the feeling you want to run away?" he asked softly as he pulled her slowly into his arms.

What might have happened next, Rachel would never know. At that very moment, Ricky's high, excited voice called, "Uncle Tony! Uncle Tony!"

The little boy came running down the stairs, shouting. "Aunt Verdonia wants to see you, Uncle Tony! You're to come up right away!"

Tony and Rachel exchanged glances. Rachel moved away, one hand ineffectively smoothing her hair in a gesture of self-conscious confusion. Tony looked slightly chagrined, but he turned, smiling, to his nephew, picked him up, and swung him around.

"Come on, Uncle Tony! Aunt Verdonia doesn't like to be kept waiting."

"Oh, she doesn't, eh? And who are you, her majesty's page summoning me to the throne room?" He set the little fellow down and met Rachel's gaze over the child's head. Rachel tried to keep her face expressionless.

Tony tickled Ricky until he collapsed in helpless giggles. Ricky righted himself, and dragging Tony by the hand, pulled him toward the staircase.

"Coming, Rachel?" Tony asked, looking back at her over his shoulder.

"In a minute." She needed to compose herself. She could not believe what had just happened, or nearly happened, between them. She took a deep breath and let it out slowly. Curious to witness the meeting between Verdonia and Tony after all these years, she hurried after the other two.

For Rachel that afternoon was like watching a scene from a drawing room farce on stage. She felt thrust into a play where everyone knew their lines except her.

Verdonia, attired in a beautiful flowered silk Japanese kimono, her hair swept up instead of hanging loose about her shoulders, was the epitome of charm as she received Tony. Rachel was amazed at the transformation from petulant invalid to gracious hostess.

To Rachel's annoyance, Tony and Verdonia attained immediate rapport. Tony was extravagantly gallant toward her and Verdonia coquettish, flirtatious.

The children, excited by the gaiety of the atmosphere and the bright conversation between their aunt and uncle, soon became over-stimulated and a little boisterous. Verdonia, however, showed not the slightest irritation and laughed along with Tony at their antics.

When it came time for Tony to leave, Verdonia said coyly, "Next time I hope to receive you properly downstairs."

"That will be my pleasure." Tony smiled, bowing over Verdonia's extended hand.

Outside in the hall, the children raced ahead of the two adults. Tony captured Rachel's hand, held it as they walked to the top of the staircase.

"That's hardly the Verdonia I recall," he said in a low voice. "If I remember correctly, Sophia's sister was not at ease socially, nor given much to chitchat. She was rather aloof, somewhat disapproving of the frivolity at the wedding festivities. But then people change. That's one of the redeeming graces of humankind. We can all change—and do." He looked at Rachel thoughtfully. "Why so pensive, Rachel?"

Again his use of her name was sweet to her ears.

"It's just that seeing someone change right before your eyes is kind of startling. That's what happened just now. You asked me before if Verdonia had been—difficult. The answer is yes, very. Yet today—the proverbial butter wouldn't melt in her mouth."

"Maybe she is getting well, feeling better. Health has a great deal to do with disposition, you know."

They had reached the bottom of the steps now, and the children were chasing each other around in the wide entry hall.

"I think I'll take the children down to the cove, let them run off some of their energy," Rachel said, deciding she should change the subject.

"I'll come with you."

"I thought you had to get back to London!" Rachel declared surprised.

"I can take a later train."

They strolled leisurely through the garden, along the path down to the sheltered beach. Late afternoon sunshine touched everything with golden light. Tony reached and took

Rachel's hand again. Feeling her palm against his, Rachel's heart warmed. For a moment she experienced a wonderful intimacy, as though she would never feel lonely again.

She chanced a sidelong glance at him. What was he feeling? He seemed lost in thought. Rachel felt a chill. He was far away, not thinking of her at all. Hadn't she cautioned herself not to take anything for granted?

The merry laughter of the children tugged at Rachel. She reminded herself Tony was her employer's brother, she the Venable children's governess. Nothing would ever bridge such social distance between them.

A feeling of loss and sadness swept over her. She disengaged her hand from Tony's and ran after the children, who had reached the water's edge, calling out to them, "Be careful!" She recognized the warning could be as much for her as for them.

*S*eemingly puzzled by her sudden coolness, Tony joined her at the water's edge. "What's the matter, Rachel?"

Her throat was sore with distress, and the threat of tears stung her eyes. Not trusting herself to speak, she simply shook her head.

He touched her arm. She moved away.

"Rachel, don't do this. Tell me. Something's wrong. I want to know what it is."

"It's just that it's impossible," she managed at last.

"What is?"

"You. Me. Oh, it's stupid. I'm just imagining."

"Uncle Tony, come see the shells I found!" Ricky shouted.

"In a minute," Tony called back.

Rachel took a few steps away, desperately trying to stem her tears.

"Rachel, wait."

He followed her, took hold of her arm, turned her around to face him. "Believe me, whatever you're feeling or thinking is *not* stupid. This is neither the time nor the place to tell you, but—"

"Uncle Tony!" Ricky's insistent voice called again.

"Rachel, come see!" Delphine's was added to her brother's.

Rachel pulled away from Tony's hold.

"The children," she reminded him.

"All right, for *now*. But later, we must talk."

They went down to where the children had scooped out a small pool in the sand and displayed the proper amount of interest and awe in the tiny sea urchins and shells they were collecting. But every once in awhile Tony's searching glance caught Rachel's and she found it difficult to turn away.

Later they walked up from the beach toward the house. The children were ahead of them on the path. Tony slipped his arm around Rachel's waist. With the other hand, he turned her face to his and kissed her.

"You shouldn't have!" she whispered.

"I've missed you," he said.

The children had rounded a curve and were momentarily out of sight. He kissed her again.

"Tony!" She quickened her step to catch up with the children. He caught her hand, held it tightly.

"I wanted you to know how I felt, Rachel."

His usual high spirits seemed revitalized. He teased and laughed and joked with the children all the rest of the way to the house.

Rachel felt as though she were moving in a dream. All her self-reminders were to no avail. At his departure, she kept the children by her side, giving Tony no opportunity to kiss her again. As he said his good-byes, his knowing gaze rested upon her with a mixture of regret and amusement. Under it, Rachel's cheeks grew warm.

In the days that followed, the kiss that hadn't happened proved as disturbing to Rachel as the one that had. The minute Tony left, she was sorry. Her emotions were like the metronome she placed on the piano when Delphine was practicing. However, the tempo of a heart was not so easily controlled as that of the musical device. One minute Rachel was ecstatic, joyous, the next bewildered, frightened. Where could it all lead?

Tony seemed totally unaware of the problem Rachel saw as insurmountable. He had gone away happy and returned the following Friday in his usual jovial mood.

They were all out on the terrace when Tony arrived. It was high summer now, warm but with a pleasant breeze. Verdonia was ensconced on the lounge chair, the children playing hopscotch. Rachel sat on a garden bench nearby. She had taken to accompanying the children when they were with Verdonia. Occupied with a book or needlework, she stayed within watching distance. Rachel knew her position as the children's governess validated her being there, even if Verdonia largely ignored her.

It may have been her presence, Rachel wasn't sure, but there were no other incidents to cause her to confront Verdonia. At least, no overt ones. However, Rachel was determined to keep her promise to Gladys should one arise.

Tony's arrival was greeted with the usual rush of enthusiasm from the children. Rachel started up then resumed her seat, wishing she had had a chance to meet Tony alone. Having him come upon her so unexpectedly, she had to control her outer reaction. She was helpless against her racing pulse, her hammering heart.

Armed with a top for Ricky, a small kaleidoscope for Dede, and flowers and a box of chocolates for Verdonia, Tony greeted everyone exuberantly, then said to Rachel, "I've wheedled Mrs. Coulter into letting me stay the weekend."

Rachel's initial delight at this announcement soon faded, however, for at the sight of Tony, Verdonia's rather sullen mood quickly changed and she eagerly attempted to monopolize Tony's attention. As Rachel went to get vases for the flowers, she wickedly defined Verdonia's sudden transformation as very much like that of a grub into a butterfly. When Rachel returned to the terrace, Verdonia, ignoring the children, was urging Tony to play picquet with her—a card game for *two* players.

"But you *must*. You can't imagine how frightfully bored I am, stuck here with no amusing company, nothing to do!"

Nothing to do but issue orders, play a tune everyone in the house has to dance to!

Verdonia shuffled the cards, all the while engaging Tony in playful conversation. Watching Tony succumb to this flirtatious manipulation, Rachel fumed silently. *Her own brother-in-law and at least twenty years younger.* But, in all fairness, Verdonia was not alone to blame. Not if Tony was taken in by her obvious flattery. Surely he wasn't that shallow or naive.

Watching them Rachel's emotions churned. She was convinced now more than ever that her attraction to Tony might doom her to disappointment and disillusionment.

Her troubled thoughts were interrupted by the appearance of Molly, the parlor maid, bearing a tray on which was a pitcher of lemonade, glasses, napkins, and a plate of cookies. She set it on a table near where Verdonia and Tony were playing cards.

"Time for a break!" Tony declared, putting down his cards.

"Just because I'm winning!" Verdonia said triumphantly. "Are you such a poor sport, then?"

"I bow to your superiority in games of chance," he replied with a grin. "Losing always makes me thirsty."

"Then once that's taken care of, will you have another round?"

"Possibly." He held out his glass.

Lured by the prospect of refreshments, the children approached the table.

A frown puckered Verdonia's brow. She poured Tony's lemonade then turned to Rachel. "Miss Penniston, see to the children. They can take their drink and cookies over there. I don't want crumbs all over our cards."

Rachel bit her lip. She glanced at Tony, thinking he would say something at Verdonia's curt directive, but he was looking at Verdonia with an unreadable expression. Admiration. Interest. Rachel couldn't tell. She was, however, furious to be treated like a servant.

She collected napkins and glasses, held out the plate of cookies for each child to take one, then walked over to the edge of the terrace and sat down on the steps with them. In a few minutes the card game recommenced, the sound of the players' bantering conversation reaching her burning ears.

Verdonia and Tony were still at it when Gladys came to take the children in for their baths. Neither Tony nor Verdonia seemed to notice when Rachel left with them. Upstairs, she told Gladys to inform the cook she would take her supper with the children that evening.

Gladys looked surprised. "Not downstairs, miss, with Miss Verdonia and Mr. Tony?"

"I have a slight headache," she fibbed. "I think I'll go to bed early."

When Rachel finally reached her bedroom, she *did* have a pounding headache. *Serves me right for lying,* she thought. She knew Tony would think it odd she didn't show up for dinner. She didn't care. It would do him good to worry. But she *did* care.

She cared *too* much about Tony Venable.

*T*he next day Rachel determined to act as naturally as possible. She knew she should try to overcome her growing aversion to Verdonia. But it was difficult. There was something about her Rachel instinctively disliked.

Rachel felt a little anxious about seeing Tony, wondering what he had made of her absence of the last evening. But when she came into the dining room for breakfast he seemed his usual pleasant self.

He greeted Rachel warmly. "Feeling better?"

"I'm fine, thank you."

"Good!" was all he said, but he regarded her intently. The thought he might suspect her motive for disappearing was jealousy made Rachel blush. She turned her back to him, helped herself to coffee at the sideboard.

He was still at the table, so she couldn't avoid joining him.

His eyes were concerned, his manner solicitous. "We missed you last night at dinner."

She sipped her coffee but did not comment.

"It was an interesting evening," he remarked, gazing steadily at Rachel. "Catching up. Or trying to. Verdonia's memory is full of holes, especially about the past, before the accident. Maybe her injuries were more serious than the doctors thought."

Rachel took a slice of toast, buttered it, and took a bite.

"She is very different than I remembered," Tony continued. "Of course, I was a mere boy. A man's perspective is not the same."

The piece of toast stuck in Rachel's throat. She reached for her coffee cup and took a sip. *Of course, a man's perspective is different than a boy's! Verdonia is an attractive woman. But she is still at least twenty years older than you, Tony Venable.*

A smile tugged the corners of Tony's mouth. Again, Rachel had the uncanny sensation he was reading her thoughts.

"Anyway, I'm glad you're up and about. I promised the children a game of croquet. They're out there now setting things up. Verdonia is willing to play, too. I told her she must start getting some exercise."

"I suppose you're an expert in such matters." Rachel's tone was arch.

Unabashed, Tony replied pleasantly, "Any good physician would say the best way to recover from an ordeal such as Verdonia underwent is to get both mind and body active."

Rachel made no further comment. Tony waited until she finished her coffee so they walked out of the dining room together.

On the smooth stretch of lawn directly in front of the terrace, Allan, the footman, was helping the children mark off the placement of the wickets. Verdonia, crisp and fresh in a pink and white striped shirtwaist with balloon sleeves, a flared skirt, and wide waist-cinching belt, turned at their approach. Ignoring Rachel, she hailed Tony. "Shall we be partners or opponents?"

"Oh, I think it should be everyone for himself. Makes the game more interesting."

The children were eager to begin. There was the customary choosing of mallets and so on. Tony flipped a coin to see who would go first. Ricky had trouble handling the mallet, too long for his height and short arms, but he valiantly struggled to manage. Delphine could not even get her ball through the first wicket. She bit her lower lip in frustration, glanced at Rachel for encouragement. In sympathy, Rachel fumbled her own initial shot and showed the little girl a better way to grip her mallet and aim.

Tony had natural athletic ability and easily played through. Verdonia showed amazing competitive spirit. Her swing was strong and sure, and her ball went sailing through the first two wickets. She triumphantly took her extra turns. It was her disregard for the children's lesser skills that irritated Rachel. When Ricky's ball was in her way of a straight shot through a wicket, Verdonia sent it sailing into the bushes with a solid whack.

She seemed to be interested only in beating Tony, who took it all as good-natured fun. When she hit *his* ball out of her line, he groaned in mock despair.

Verdonia laughed loudly. "Fair's fair!" She raised her mallet in a triumphant wave declaring, "I won, I won!"

She dropped her mallet carelessly, and linking arms with Tony suggested, "Let's have some refreshment, Tony." Together they walked back onto the terrace, where fruit juice and tea service had been placed under the umbrellaed table.

Rachel looked after them resentfully. The children had not had much fun at all. A game that should have been geared to their enjoyment had become a test of Verdonia's prowess. She had certainly gained back her strength, Rachel thought grudgingly.

To make up for Ricky and Delphine's obvious disappointment, Rachel played another game with them. It was slow going, and her annoyance with the other adults mounted. They were sitting in the shade, laughing and talking and enjoying themselves thoroughly.

She had expected better of Tony.

Her resentful thoughts were interrupted by Tony's calling, "Come and join us, Rachel, and bring the children."

Ricky immediately let go of his mallet and ran up the terrace steps. Delphine glanced questioningly at Rachel. There seemed nothing else to do but go.

Rachel busied herself pouring juice into tumblers for the children, which they drank thirstily. Then they asked to be excused and ran back to play a kind of croquet game of their own devising, leaving Rachel troubled and uncomfortable.

Verdonia was in the middle of a long, funny story, directing the telling of it to Tony. Sitting opposite her, Rachel examined her own antagonistic feelings for Verdonia. Rachel certainly had meant to carry out Mr. Venable's request to make his sister-in-law comfortable, content here at Talisman. But all Verdonia's actions had made this difficult for her to do.

Rachel tried to remember her early impressions of Verdonia. Her first was that of an arresting beauty, not classically so, but rather intriguingly, a face demanding attention, one with a chameleon quality. At first she had seemed pale, fragile, withdrawn. Today, just the opposite. She seemed lively, glowing, energetic.

Was it jealousy that made her so critical of Verdonia? Certainly Tony's flattering attention to Verdonia galled Rachel. Undeniably Verdonia was clever and witty. However, Rachel found Verdonia's wit cutting. Her stories about people often contained disparaging barbs, and her gift of mimicry was sometimes cruelly used. Finally, it was how she had dealt with the children that had turned Rachel against her. Verdonia seemed to delight in the kind of malicious teasing Rachel abhorred.

Suddenly Rachel became conscious of Tony's gaze upon her. She wondered if he guessed how she felt. Pretending to wipe up a spill Ricky had made, she averted her face away from his penetrating regard.

Just then, Molly, the parlor maid, came to the terrace door. Looking confused and worried, she beckoned Rachel, who rose immediately and went over to her.

"Beg pardon, miss," Molly said. "A gentleman's jest come. He sez he's from the railroad company. He sez he understood this was the residence of Miss Verdonia Templeton. He sez he must see her."

"Did you tell Mrs. Coulter?"

"I did, miss, but she's lyin' down and sez you were to handle it."

"Where is he?"

"In the morning room, miss. I didn't know where else to have him wait."

"All right. Thank you, Molly."

Rachel followed the maid into the house, across the hall to the small reception room.

There she found a tall man, hands clasped behind his back, looking out through the French windows onto the terrace where Verdonia, Tony, and the children presented as pleasant a scene as might be viewed through a stereopticon.

The man, neatly dressed in a belted tweed suit, turned and stepped forward. He had a commanding presence, and he towered over Rachel. When he spoke his voice had the slight defining burr of a Scotsman. "Good afternoon, Miss Templeton?"

"I'm not Miss Templeton," Rachel replied. "I'm Miss Penniston, the governess here. The housekeeper, Mrs. Coulter, usually sees to tradesmen, the ordering of supplies and so on; however, today she is unwell and asked me to see you. How can I help you, sir?"

A slight sardonic smile lifted the corners of his mouth under a well-shaped mustache. His eyes were the cold, clear blue of a highland trout stream.

"I'm not a tradesman, Miss Penniston. I'm Inspector Ross Sinclair." He handed her a small business card.

Rachel read it and was embarrassed to see it identified him as an investigator for the railroad line.

"I'm representing the company in the matter of the train wreck six weeks ago. I have been assigned to trace some of the victims of the accident and interview them regarding what they can remember about the accident."

///

"Miss Templeton has only recently been released from the hospital. She is still recuperating from the effects of the accident," Rachel said. "I'm not sure she is up to being interviewed, Inspector."

"Perhaps I could speak to the lady herself?" Inspector Sinclair spoke quietly but firmly. "I assure you it will take only a few minutes of her time."

Rachel got the impression he was used to being in command of any given situation and did not easily accept a refusal. Still she hesitated.

"You may not understand, Miss Penniston, the importance that our investigation move forward as quickly as possible." He paused. "Many of the bodies remain unidentified, their luggage unclaimed. Among some of the luggage retrieved from the wreckage were several pieces initialed VT and tagged as belonging to a Miss Verdonia Templeton, destination listed as Talisman in the village of Craigburne. In order for these to be returned to her, she must make positive identification, in the presence of witnesses, and verify the contents inspected for any damage or loss that might be claimed by her."

He paused again, as if to be sure Rachel was getting the point. "Since I've brought these pieces along for Miss Templeton to identify, I will be as brief as I can. I would like to interview her today and give her the opportunity to reclaim her belongings."

His tone brooked no opposition. There was really nothing Rachel could do but agree.

"I suppose it will be all right. She is outside on the terrace. If you explain why you've come, I think she will understand the necessity and will be willing to cooperate. Please come with me."

As Rachel escorted the inspector out onto the terrace, she saw Verdonia had moved over to the chaise and Tony was leaning toward her. They were both laughing. As Rachel approached with the inspector, Verdonia looked up, annoyed. Her eyes narrowed as Rachel introduced him.

"This is Inspector Sinclair, an investigator from the railroad. He's come to ask you a few questions about the accident."

Even as Rachel spoke, the laughter died away and Verdonia's smile faded. She visibly paled, sank back into her recliner. A look of horror passed over her face, and she put up one arm as though to ward off a blow.

"I feel faint," Verdonia murmured.

Alarmed, Rachel rushed over to her. She picked up Verdonia's limp wrist and chafed it gently.

"I'll get some brandy!" Tony said and sprang to his feet. He brushed by the inspector and hurried into the house.

"I was afraid this would be too much for her," Rachel said to Inspector Sinclair. "She hates to talk about the wreck."

The inspector did not respond, just stood by patiently as Tony came back with a decanter in one hand and a small glass in the other. After pouring it half full, he held it to Verdonia's mouth.

The children had stopped playing and stood, open mouthed, eyes wide, silently watching the drama unfolding in front of them.

Verdonia coughed but held the glass, took another swallow, then leaned back against the chaise cushions.

"I'm sorry to upset you, madam. But it is important we have this information. The railroad company is preparing a report for the insurance adjusters, and we need to have as complete a statement from each survivor as possible."

"It's just that it brings back such awful memories," Verdonia said weakly.

"Must you do this today, Inspector?" Rachel asked.

"If Miss Templeton is willing, we can get this over quickly."

Again Rachel had the impression he was a man not easily swayed from his objectives.

"Just thinking about it brings it all back," Verdonia declared with a shudder, sighing dramatically. "I don't think I'm able to talk about it." She shook her head, closed her eyes. "I'm experiencing vertigo!"

Inspector Sinclair seemed unmoved by her distress. He simply maintained his silence and waited for Verdonia to regain her composure.

"Perhaps you should talk about it," Rachel urged her gently.

"Oh, very well. Let us be done with it." Verdonia drained the brandy glass and sat up. Rachel pushed a pillow behind her back. Tony stood to one side.

"I'll have my assistant bring in the luggage, and we can dispense with this in short order." Inspector Sinclair walked briskly around the terrace to the front of the house.

"Still feeling faint, Verdonia? Perhaps another brandy?"

She seemed to be about to take Tony's suggestion, but just then Inspector Sinclair returned, accompanied by a man he introduced as his assistant, Mr. Fuller, who pushed a small handcart on which were piled a number of traveling bags.

"These came from the same compartment as the one indicated on your ticket, Miss Templeton. I gather someone else shared it. Do you remember that person? Or what kind of luggage was theirs? Maybe not all of these pieces are yours. However, I brought all of them for purposes of identification."

There were two worn leather bags plastered with stickers from foreign countries and cities, as though the owner had been a great traveler. These pieces Verdonia quickly denied. Then a trio of handsome calf suitcases initialed with the gilt letters VT were displayed along with an alligator jewel and toilette case, also monogrammed.

"Would you have a key, Miss Templeton?" Inspector Sinclair asked.

Verdonia looked blank. "You mean these have not been opened?"

"They were locked. It was assumed the owner had the key on her person or in her handbag."

"Of course. Things have been rather vague for me since the accident. I had a concussion. My handbag must be upstairs in my room."

"Would you like me to get it for you?" Rachel offered.

Verdonia frowned for a second, then turned to Ricky.

"Ricky, sweetie, you know where auntie's handbag is, don't you? In the drawer of the table beside my bed?"

Delighted to be the center of adult attention, Ricky ran to Verdonia. She patted his shoulder. "*He* can run up and get it for me so we can find the key to open my bags. There's a dear boy."

It took Ricky but a few minutes to run up and come back down. Panting but flushed with success, he handed Verdonia the handbag.

Rachel's glance met Tony's. Something curious flickered in his eyes, and something passed between them, unspoken yet very real. Rachel felt sure Tony was thinking the same thing. Verdonia did not want Rachel to fetch her handbag. Did not trust her to do so. Rachel blinked and turned away.

The handbag produced a small key ring with several dangling keys. Verdonia had to try a number of them to find the right ones to unlatch the two larger bags. Her hand trembled noticeably. Rachel felt an unexpected sympathy. However she personally felt about her, Verdonia had been through a horrifying experience, and it was obvious this was bringing it all back in vivid detail.

Opened, the bags were filled with carefully packed clothes of good taste, expensive materials, and fine workmanship. Verdonia identified them as hers. The toilette case contained such basic toiletries as complexion soap, face cream, hand lotion, nail file and buffer, bath salts and powder, an ivory-rimmed hand mirror, two hairbrushes, and a box of tortoise shell hairpins.

The suede-lined jewelry case had surprisingly little in it, a diamond *fleur de lis* pin, a gold chain, a necklace of amber beads, an ornamental marquisette hair comb, silver shoe buckles. There was a small, separate velvet pouch containing a string of matinee length pearls. There was an empty niche the size of a lady's fob watch. Verdonia said she had worn the watch traveling and it had been lost in the accident.

"Everything else then is accounted for, Miss Templeton?" Inspector Sinclair asked when the missing watch had been explained.

"Yes, Inspector."

"And I assume you have no memory of who might have been in the compartment with you at the time of the wreck, to whom these other bags might belong."

"I told you, Inspector, my memory is one of the most distressing things about my injuries—" Verdonia's voice shook with fatigue.

"Very well, I suppose I shall just have to continue searching for the owner. I thank you for your cooperation. Good day to you all." The inspector bowed slightly and, unsmiling, walked back to the house, followed by his assistant pushing the handcart filled with the much-traveled, unclaimed baggage.

After Inspector Sinclair's departure, Verdonia rose from the chaise. "Having to dredge up that awful experience has exhausted me. I think I'll have to go rest." She swayed slightly, and Tony offered his arm solicitously. "Here, Verdonia."

She slipped her hand through his arm, saying to Rachel, "Have my supper sent up on a tray."

Rachel watched them walk into the house, Verdonia leaning on Tony, her head almost resting on his shoulder. The inspector's visit had certainly affected Verdonia.

With Verdonia taking to her bed for the evening and Mrs. Coulter still keeping to her room, Rachel looked forward to having dinner alone with Tony. Maybe she could share some of her troubling thoughts.

The children were flushed, their clothes wrinkled and grass stained. Rachel took them upstairs so they could bathe and change. Leaving Gladys to supervise, Rachel hurried back down the steps, hoping to find Tony on the terrace after escorting Verdonia to her suite. She found him in the downstairs hall, standing by the open front door, apparently in deep thought.

"Tony." He turned around. Slowly his serious expression softened, and he smiled.

"Quite a day, wouldn't you say?"

"Indeed. Tony, there's something I need to talk to you about."

He frowned, pulled out his pocket watch. "Can it wait, Rachel? I've asked Melton to bring the carriage around to take me to the station."

"But why? I thought you were going to stay the weekend." She knew her dismay was apparent.

"Something's come up. I've got to get back to London."

Tony seemed preoccupied, a little distracted. Unable to stop herself Rachel asked, "But when will you be down again?"

"Oh, well—I'm not sure. I'll send word."

"That's *it?* What shall I tell the children?"

He stared at her for a moment, as if he hadn't quite heard her. "The children? Just say—whatever you think."

"It must be something pretty important for you to rush away like this." She knew she was revealing her disappointment, but she couldn't help it.

Tony frowned. "It *is* important, Rachel. I can't tell you exactly but—"

"Important as an embassy ball, perhaps?" she asked.

Surprised, as if he had just become aware her feelings were hurt, Tony leaned forward, but she stepped back.

"Ah, Rachel, don't—"

Rachel turned away stiffly. She felt abandoned but was too proud to confess that and ask him to stay.

Tony seemed about to say something else, but Melton appeared at the front door. "We'll have to leave now, sir, or you'll miss your train."

"I must go, Rachel. I can't explain but please try to understand—"

"But I *don't* understand."

"Sir," Melton warned again.

"Good-bye, Rachel." Tony gave her a regretful glance and was out the door.

Rachel dined alone in the huge dining room, feeling worse than ever. As she toyed with her food, the afternoon with Inspector Sinclair played back in her mind like shifting scenes in a magic lantern show. There had been something disturbing about his visit. At one point, her glance had met his, and something intangible passed between them. What had she seen in his eyes? Suspicion, guardedness, skepticism? His business was investigation. That took special skills of observation and detection. How many of this type of investigation had he done? How many were involved in this one train accident alone?

She had read there had been looting at the wreck site before the police had been able to set up postings. Rescue workers and others had gone in to search for and drag out the abandoned luggage of the injured as well as of the casualties. Badly injured people had had no thoughts of their belongings as they were carried to safety. Valuables of all kinds had been left in the wreckage, to be later sorted, tagged, categorized, and the legitimate owners located. Perhaps that's why the inspector had seemed to scrutinize Verdonia so closely as she unpacked, looked through her suitcases, and checked the contents of her jewelry case. It was his job.

At another point during the proceedings Rachel had been struck by the way Tony was regarding Verdonia. Had he been sympathizing with her for having to go through another ordeal? Maybe it was better Tony had left, whatever his reason. Maybe it was not a good idea to discuss her feelings about Verdonia with him. She was, after all, his brother's sister-in-law. To confide she found Verdonia unlikeable, with traits of spitefulness and furtiveness that made Rachel uneasy, might be a mistake.

Better to keep her own counsel. Do her job. However, Verdonia's dealings with the children were another matter. The children's happiness and welfare were *her* responsibility. She would be failing in her duty if she did not discuss the favoritism and teasings. She wouldn't let it go on even if it meant confronting Verdonia.

Rachel pushed her chair away from the table, and leaving her dessert untasted, flung down her napkin and left the dining room. The house was quiet as she slowly mounted the stairway. She looked in on the children, both sound asleep, then went to her own bedroom.

In the midweek's post, Rachel received a note from Tony. She could tell from the handwriting it was written in haste, and it certainly did not contain what she wanted to hear.

"My dear Rachel. Circumstances have made it impossible for me to come to Talisman this coming weekend. I'll be out of communication for a while. I'll explain when I see you, though I cannot say exactly when that will be. Please know you are often in my thoughts. I look forward to being with you as soon as I can. Yours, Tony."

Rachel tore it up. She felt frustrated, angry even. Although she knew it wasn't Tony's fault he served at the pleasure of the embassy official for whom he was an aide. He had explained that often diplomatic crises came up unexpectedly and trips were hastily arranged. It was all very secretive and obscure. One part of her understood that. The other part felt forsaken.

The next few days Rachel felt depressed. She woke up each morning almost unwilling to face her day. It was not like her at all. She had always been an even-tempered, optimistic, person. Rachel tried to shake off her heaviness of spirit, but much as she fought against it, everything she did seemed an effort. Ever since Verdonia had come, a smothering pall had hung over Talisman.

London

A muggy, overcast day, heat rose through the city, making it hard to breathe. Tony hurried along on his mission. He wasn't quite sure what he hoped to find, even what he was looking for, but he had decided to check the nagging doubts in his mind. Had to start somewhere.

The morgue of the London *Daily Times* newspaper was down two dusty flights of circular stairs in a subterranean room. Light filtered in, pale shafts from narrow windows spaced widely apart. In one corner, a bespectacled man with a thatch of tousled rusty gray hair sat at a desk, bending over a large open scrapbook. He dipped a brush into a pot of white paste, spread glue onto the pages, meticulously affixed strips of newsprint. Behind him were shelves of mottled blue cardboard file boxes.

He raised his head slowly, squinting up through wire-framed glasses at Tony, pointed with a crooked finger to a shelf with stacks of the same kind of scrapbook on which he was working. "They're arranged, labeled by month, date, and year," he said in a croaky voice. "Makes it easy to find the copy of the newspaper you're looking for and read it."

Tony thanked him and made a quick tour of the shelves. Locating the one he wanted, he lifted it down and brought it to one of four long, narrow tables with straight chairs placed in front of the shelves. He spread the scrapbook out flat so he could turn the pages freely. He turned the stiffened pages, hunting for the report. His index finger moved along the columns of type as rapidly as his eyes scanned the text. At length, he found the day's news he wanted, its banner headline fairly leaping out at him.

Quickly he read the account, then sat for a few minutes, absorbing the details of the reporter's story:

Many of the survivors taken from the scene were dazed, incoherent, unable to relate what had happened to them or their fellow passengers. Local hospitals were not capable of handling the numerous casualties, so some were taken by ambulance as far as London, where they were placed in hospices and nursing homes. Luggage, belongings, clothing were strewn everywhere. This reporter saw such odd unrelated things as an umbrella, a lady's bonnet, a child's rag doll.

Railroad crews worked diligently through the night, removing the twisted metal and steel of the wreckage. Authorities said it would probably take weeks before a thorough investigation could determine conclusively the cause of the accident and confirm passengers accounted for, belongings restored.

Tony frowned. Something formless pushed to be acknowledged in his mind. Vague, tenuous, puzzling. He could not seem to grasp it, except to feel its urgency. He returned the heavy scrapbook to the shelf and walked slowly along the row of shelves, not quite sure what he was looking for. Was it when he was at Oxford? Or before that when he was a fifteen-year-old schoolboy? It would be like looking for a needle in a haystack if he couldn't remember.

Leaving the newspaper morgue, he returned to his London flat. He felt strangely restless but weary. He stretched out on his bed, and in spite of all his conflicting thoughts he drifted, on the verge of sleep.

Then quite suddenly he found himself fully awake. He sat bolt upright, completely alert. *That* was it. He realized what it was that disturbed him most about Verdonia Templeton.

Ten years can make a great deal of difference in someone's appearance, especially a woman of Verdonia's age. But there were other things that could not be as easily dismissed. Still, he could be mistaken.

He jumped up, grabbed his coat, and went out again. The afternoon was waning, the streets clogged with traffic.

He must hurry before the newspaper morgue closed.

13

he first week in August the weather turned uncomfortably warm. Talisman, set back as it was in a copse and surrounded by high walls and the maze, did not get the cooling winds from the ocean. The mugginess made the children lethargic, the servants indolent. It added to Rachel's feelings of depression. The heavy atmosphere seemed to have an effect on everyone. Except Verdonia.

With the arrival of her trunks, suitcases, and other belongings, Verdonia seemed energized. Although she still had breakfast in bed, her mornings were spent trying on different outfits. She changed several times a day, wearing different combinations of dresses and hats.

One day, passing Verdonia's bedroom, Rachel noticed the door was ajar. She looked in and saw Verdonia surveying herself in the full-length mirror, clad only in her chemise and pantaloons, her shoulders and arms bare. Rachel was astonished.

Where Rachel had assumed Verdonia was merely thin, her body was lithe and muscular. Moreover, Rachel was convinced Verdonia employed cosmetics. Her complexion, no longer pale and sallow, was definitely pink. Her eyes, in themselves quite lovely, a smoky blue, were enhanced, outlined and darkened with kohl. Her hair shone with auburn lights. Artificial ones, Rachel knew, because Verdonia had sent Molly, the parlor maid, to the village chemist shop to buy her henna to tint her hair.

It was all pretty shocking. Maybe in Canada and America it was accepted for ladies to use such enhancing devices, but in England it was generally frowned on.

Verdonia had become a real puzzle to Rachel. Sometimes Rachel lay awake at night thinking about how the woman had seemed to change before her eyes. At first Verdonia seemed merely temperamental, due, Rachel thought, to her accident. Lately she had become unimaginably difficult.

Awaking early one morning unable to sleep more, Rachel got up, dressed, and slipped out of the house for a long walk on the grounds. As she walked she reviewed all the startling changes Verdonia had wrought at Talisman.

Verdonia was now flagrantly arrogant, usurping Mrs. Coulter's authority, countermanding the housekeeper's orders, changing the menus at whim, altering established routines with her requests. She treated Molly as her personal attendant, sending her off to the village milliner for puggrees, to the fabric store for lace and trims to freshen up her rather plain blouses, to the candy store for her favorite bonbons.

This sent Mrs. Coulter into a tizzy. She complained to Rachel that Verdonia disrupted the household routine, caused Molly to neglect her duties. Mrs. Coulter sniffed disdainfully at the fripperies Verdonia sent Molly to buy. "Downright Dolly Vardenish!" she declared. "Cheap, flashy, and in poor taste."

Rachel found it hard to remember what it was like before Verdonia Templeton came. Those happy days of early summer had faded as if they had never been. Before Verdonia's arrival, Rachel had loved her job; now she looked forward to her days off. Until Verdonia came, she had loved everything about Talisman, so much so that even at times she had stayed away only long enough to accomplish a few errands, happy to return to its gracious welcome. Now all that had changed.

On her days off, Rachel browsed in the bookstore or tried on bonnets or passed the time at the notions counter of the fabric store looking at wheels of ribbons, laces, or trimmings, stretching out the afternoon, delaying her return to Talisman as long as possible. Even when she should have been enjoying herself, though she found she could not help worrying about what might be going on while she was gone. And she had an uneasiness about leaving the children too long, especially if they were with Verdonia when she left.

Thoughts of Tony also filled her mind. She missed him more than she allowed herself to admit. She knew she had let her feelings go too far. It was foolish of her to even dream of such a love. It was completely out of the question and not at all the way Rachel had imagined falling in love would be. She had not imagined this many obstacles to a possible happy ending.

What she *had* imagined was completely unrealistic. A love story she had told herself. The man in the dream would be a poet or a musician or a composer, someone not bound by the rigid social codes of their day. Someone with whom she could escape to a faraway, romantic place, maybe an enchanted Greek isle where they would live in a seaside cottage, sit in a courtyard shaded by an arbor of gnarled vines, the scent of lemons on the warm air. The trouble was her *imagined* lover now had Tony Venable's face!

Silly, romantic fool, she chastised herself. Tossing her head as if to shake it free of dreams, Rachel scolded herself. While she was romanticizing about him, Tony most certainly was not thinking of her. The brief messages scrawled on postcards were hardly love letters. Out of sight, out of mind was probably more true than not, as far as Tony was concerned. Forget this foolishness, Rachel ordered herself. Depend on yourself. Stop wasting your time on dreams that can't come true. Even as she lectured herself, thoughts of Tony remained. His warmth, his laughter, his way with the children had all endeared him to her—way too much.

On Rachel's next afternoon off, prompted by some vague feeling she ought to get back to Talisman, she cut her idle window-shopping short. Instead of treating herself to a leisurely tea at the Harbor Inn, she made an about-face and started toward Talisman.

Although Rachel did not believe in hunches or premonitions, she felt a needling to get back to the house as soon as possible. She hurried along the road from town, trying to calm her rising disquiet.

She had gone only a short way when quite suddenly the sky overhead clouded, the day darkened mysteriously. Soon she felt a few sprinkles. Why had she not brought a parasol with her? The air *smelled* like rain. More was sure to come. Rachel walked a little faster.

Just as she turned in to the country lane that led to Talisman, it began to drizzle. She quickened her pace again. Could she make it to shelter before it began to rain hard?

Through a thin veil of rain she saw the hazy outline of Talisman. It would have been natural for her to hurry. Strangely, though, her steps lagged. As she approached the gates, she felt a curious reluctance to enter them. Something almost physical held her back, in direct conflict with her sense of persistent urgency. A sense of foreboding enveloped her. Was it one of the children? The closer she got to the house the more depressed she felt. Usually it seemed a beautiful place, stones gleaming in the sunlight, the stained glass windows shining like jewels. Now it seemed threatening.

She pressed on, fighting the dread. Still something told her she must hurry. A clap of thunder was followed by a clattering of rain that drenched her jacket, soaked her skirt. A strong wind blew against her back, driving her forward.

Picking up her sodden hem, she rushed up the drive and stumbled up the shallow steps onto the terrace. Her bonnet was soaked, her hair streaming wet from beneath it, plastered against her forehead. She stopped for a minute, grabbing hold of one of the wrought iron chairs to catch her breath.

Then panic overcame her. A terrible need to get to the children, to see if they were all right. She ran into the house and up the stairs, breathlessly clinging to the banister. At the landing, her side was aching, her breath coming in short gasps. She hurried down the hall to the children's room, hoping against hope her intuition was wrong.

Bursting into the nursery she found Delphine in a near-hysterical state, a startled Gladys trying to comfort her. At the sight of Rachel, the little girl threw herself into her arms, sobbing. Over her head Rachel looked at Gladys. "What is it? What happened?"

"I don't know exactly what 'appened, miss, 'cept Miss Dede came arunnin' from Miss Verdonia's room in tears." The maid's mouth curled contemptuously. "Probably said sumpin' out of turn or didn't hop when *she* said to! I'm sure I couldn't say."

"Darling, do you want to tell me about it?" Rachel asked softly, cradling the child tenderly against her. The sobs slowed to hiccups, and finally out spilled a long, involved tale of a misunderstood direction, a sharp reprimand. Then when Delphine went to do her aunt's bidding, she jiggled the small table and the house of cards Verdonia and Ricky were building collapsed. A tongue-lashing followed. Weeping, Delphine ran out of the room. That was when Gladys had found her.

"Well, it's all right now, darling. I'll speak to your aunt, explain you didn't mean to upset their game. It will be all right, I promise," Rachel told her soothingly.

"Gladys, do fix Miss Delphine some cocoa and open that tin of cookies Tony brought last time. I've got to get out of these clothes. I got rained on coming back from the village."

Rachel turned back to Dede. "Afterward, we'll have a story, how's that?"

The little girl seemed better, so Rachel went to change out of her rain-soaked clothes. All the while she tried to calm her fury. How could Verdonia be so thoughtless? Didn't she realize what a vulnerable, sensitive child Delphine was? To fly into a rage over something so trivial, to frighten the little girl to tears, was inexcusable.

Although outwardly calm, inside Rachel was seething. She knew she could no longer put off the confrontation with Verdonia. There had been too many incidents of favoritism, spitefulness. She was determined to put a stop to it.

After the children were in bed, Rachel garnered her resolve, went down the hall, and tapped at Verdonia's sitting room door. Verdonia was at the dressing table buffing her nails and looked up boredly at Rachel's entrance.

While Rachel explained as tactfully as she could the reason for her visit, Verdonia's eyes narrowed, then flashed with anger. Her face flooded with ugly, red blotches. Then she exploded.

"And who came tale-bearing such nonsense to you, Miss Penniston? That little sneak of a maid, Gladys? She's always hanging about, *spying* on me. Well, I'll have no more of it. She should be sent packing."

Rachel was too shocked by this outburst to react. Then just as suddenly, Verdonia's tone changed. She raised her eyebrows as if in astonishment.

"That maid has blown it way out of proportion. I may have jestingly said something the child misunderstood, but it was nothing. I'm astonished you'd even bring it up, Miss Penniston. Surely you realize in your capacity as their governess that Delphine is highly emotional and takes offense at the slightest thing."

She shrugged and resumed manicuring her nails, indicating she was not going to discuss the matter further.

Rachel made one more attempt. "Delphine *is* extremely sensitive, Miss Templeton. We all try to be careful of her feelings."

Verdonia tossed the nail buffer down. "She's spoiled, pampered! *That's* what's wrong with her. Well, I'm not catering to a child's *delicate* thin skin! Now, that's it, Miss Penniston. Good night."

Rachel, taken aback by the woman's lack of compassion, wanted to come to Dede's defense, but she knew it was useless. Verdonia refused to listen. Frustrated, dismissed, Rachel left. When Verdonia was in a less volatile mood, Rachel was determined to broach the subject of the wedge built between the children by Verdonia's favoring Ricky over Delphine.

The next day Verdonia made a great show of being sweet to Delphine in front of Rachel and Gladys. "What a silly little goose, you are," she said reaching out and bringing Delphine close to her. "Such a ninny to get all upset at your auntie. Ricky never does, and neither must you—if you want auntie to love you!"

She then playfully pinched Dede's cheek. Rachel saw the little girl wince and her big eyes fill with sudden tears. The pinch had hurt. Had it been meant to?

Enraged by what she suspected, Rachel made it a point to go back to Verdonia that very afternoon. "I must speak to you, Miss Templeton."

"What is it now?" Verdonia demanded with an exasperated sigh.

Rachel tried to explain about the growing signs of jealousy between the brother and sister.

Verdonia flushed. "Just who do you think you are, Miss Penniston? I don't know on what credentials my brother-in-law hired you, but as far as I'm concerned you are overstepping your place by telling me how to treat my nephew and niece. It's a tempest in a teapot, and the subject is closed. You would do well to remember that I am in charge here now."

Rachel did not miss the implied threat in Verdonia's words. Infuriated but realizing that saying more could be disastrous, Rachel left, but she was determined to be even more watchful and protective of the children.

14

*R*achel deliberately planned excursions for the children that kept them away from Verdonia. That was no problem for Delphine, who avoided Verdonia anyway. But Ricky, still in his aunt's favor, enjoyed the candy and pampering he got in exchange for running errands and carrying messages to the kitchen for special treats, which he got to share.

The first week in September afforded Rachel the opportunity to get both children away from the house and Verdonia for a full day. A shopping trip to outfit them for the coming winter was proposed by Mrs. Coulter, and Rachel would take them. That meant a short train trip to the next town where the stores were larger and ready-made clothing was available. The children were excited about the adventure the day promised. Rachel was happy to see their old easy camaraderie reassert itself as they went to the village, boarded the train, settled in the compartment for the brief ride to Marismead.

Remembering what an appealing little boy Ricky had been when she first came to Talisman—before Verdonia's arrival— Rachel was filled with rage at how their aunt had destroyed the harmonious relationship between brother and sister. Well, today would be a pleasant break for all of them.

After trying on numerous jackets and caps and being fitted for two pairs of shoes each, the children were ready for the treat Rachel had promised. Purchases made, boxed, and packaged, they headed out of the store on their way for a special tea.

They started down to the main street, Ricky and Dede running ahead of Rachel, stopping every once in a while to press their noses against shop windows or to point out some fascinating display to each other. All at once, from behind her, Rachel heard her name spoken.

She turned around and was surprised to see none other than Inspector Sinclair. He took off his hat and bowed slightly. "Miss Penniston. What an unexpected pleasure to see you again. A surprise to see you here in Marismead."

That sounded more a question than a statement. Impulsively, Rachel explained how she happened to be in Marismead. A minute later, she realized that had not been necessary. All she should have done was acknowledge him and move on. But somehow she felt he had something more to say to her, something she should hear.

"I could say the same for you, Inspector. I thought you worked out of London."

"I am continuing my investigation of the survivors of the railroad accident. Marismead was one of several stops after Craigburne. Some passengers and baggage remain unaccounted for, information to be collected." He paused. "And how is Miss Templeton? Fully recovered by now? Some of the baggage found in her compartment is still unclaimed. I would certainly like to know if and what she can remember about anyone who shared her compartment. Do you think possibly she is well enough for me to question her again?"

Rachel started to say Verdonia seemed perfectly fine, then stopped herself. It wasn't *her* place to give the inspector permission to call on her again. As she hesitated, he regarded her with interest.

"I really couldn't say, Inspector," Rachel said, aware of her awkward situation. If she indicated to him that was an option, and the inspector were to come unannounced and unexpected and mention Rachel had led him to believe it would be all right, *she* would be blamed. She would surely bear the brunt of Verdonia's wrath. Better not. Her situation was precarious enough as it was with Verdonia. She couldn't risk being sent packing, having to abandon her charges.

The children were getting too far ahead down the street.

"I'm sorry, I really must go," Rachel said quickly, taking a step away. "I promised the children a treat before getting the train back to Craigburne."

"That sounds delightful." Inspector Sinclair nodded approvingly. Then he took out a card case, removed a card, and handed it to her. "My card, Miss Penniston. If anything comes up you think would help in our investigation, I can be reached at either home or office, at any time."

She took the card and dropped in into her handbag.

"Come on, Miss Rachel!" Ricky's shrill little voice called, and Delphine motioned impatiently.

Inspector Sinclair lifted his hat. "Good day, Miss Penniston."

Rachel hurried after the children, who had almost reached the tea shop at the corner. What a strange coincidence, running into Inspector Sinclair like that! His expression, while impassive, still had a look as though—as though what? There had been something penetrating about his gray eyes. What was he trying to find out from *her* about Verdonia? Did he suspect Verdonia was concealing something? But what? About another passenger in her compartment? And why?

Rachel hurried to catch up with the children, putting aside her troubling questions.

In the bakery shop, customers selected their treat from a cart wheeled around to each table. Ricky wanted everything, and Rachel had to make him choose. While Delphine was taking a deliberate time to make her choice, the waitress addressed Rachel.

"These are the Venable children, from over at Talisman in Craigburne, aren't they? So Mr. Venable is off to Australia. Came into a fortune, did he?"

Taken aback at first, Rachel realized in small towns, families visited back and forth. The gentry were always topics of gossip. The children had been born and grew up nearby so naturally they would be recognized. That Mr. Venable was away and *she* was the governess had probably also been discussed.

Rachel darted a quick look at the children, but they were deciding between decorated cakes and raspberry puffs dusted with powdered sugar. The woman expected an answer, so Rachel said quietly, "Well, he's gone to see about some property."

The woman made no effort to lower her voice. "The way I heard it, it's thousands of acres of land and sheep, and some say, even gold mines. Well, them that has, gits, I always say! Life's not fair in doling out the wealth, that's for sure."

Rachel felt the curious glances of other tea shop customers upon them, heard the hum of conversation at the nearby tables lower to a murmur.

"I guess *his* young ones'll be as rich as the queen's children some day."

Rachel looked around uneasily. She heartily wished they had chosen the other tea shop for their treat. The children seemed oblivious to the exchange that had taken place about them, but Rachel was glad when they finished their tea and left the shop. She tried to tell herself ignorant people were careless in their talk; however, the incident left an uneasy residue in her mind. What other rumors were circulating in the town about Talisman?

The children, worn out by the time they boarded the train for the return trip, curled up on either side of Rachel and fell asleep. When they pulled into Craigburne station, Ricky woke up predictably cranky. Melton was there with the carriage to meet them and drive them back to Talisman. He seemed particularly taciturn to Rachel. She chalked it up to the train being nearly ten minutes late and his possibly having to wait a long time for them.

As soon as they arrived home, Rachel realized the true reason for the man's ill humor. Talisman's orderly routine had once again been turned upside down.

15

*T*he minute they stepped inside, they heard voices and laughter. Dede looked up at Rachel. "Do you think Uncle Tony's here with Aunt Verdonia?"

Tony? Rachel's heart leaped. Oh, how she hoped so.

Immediately, Ricky roused himself. His sleepiness vanished. Both children tugged at Rachel's hands, dragging her toward the drawing room. She let herself be pulled, then at the threshold they stopped short.

Instead of Tony, a strange man was seated on the sofa with Verdonia. Dressed in a flashy suit of gold-green and mustard plaid, he leaned back against the pillows, smoking a long cigar. On the table in front of them was a decanter of wine. It was he who saw the three of them standing in the doorway. Halting, mid-sentence, he stared back at them. "Well, well!" he drawled, blowing out a puff of smoke.

Verdonia turned her head and saw them. A frown replaced her smile.

"Oh, it's *you!*" She spoke with obvious irritation. "You're back early, aren't you?" Not waiting for a reply, she said, "This is my cousin, Leo Erwin. Down from London."

137

The man put down his half-empty wine glass, got to his feet, and made a sweeping bow.

"At your service," he said with an ingratiating smile. "And who might these delightful youngsters be, my dear?"

Verdonia waved an indifferent hand. "Venable's children, Delphine and Derrick."

"And the charming young lady?" he persisted, his rather protuberant eyes studying Rachel, much to her annoyance.

Just then Ricky broke loose from her hold and ran over to Verdonia.

"I didn't know we had a cousin Leo." Ricky tilted his head to look up at the stranger. "Papa never told us about you," he declared.

The man glanced at Verdonia, then grinned down at the little boy. "Your father doesn't know all about *our side* of the family."

"Are you from Canada, too?"

"Not recently. But I've been there. I've been all over, if the truth were told. Germany and France, New Zealand and Australia—"

"Australia!" both children exclaimed in unison. "That's where Papa is!"

Delphine, now intrigued, moved tentatively into the room.

"Well, now is that a fact or not! It's a small world I always say, wouldn't you?" He chuckled and patted Ricky on the head. "Why, I just came back from one of my travels and found out—just by chance, you might say—that my dear cousin was here in jolly old England. Of course, I had to come down and pay my respects. We're having a fine time catchin' up with each other." He smiled and winked at Verdonia.

"Miss Penniston, I think you should take the children upstairs. Gladys has been worried; they're late for their tea."

Rachel wondered if Verdonia realized she was contradicting her previous remark that they were *early*.

"Yes, of course. Come, children." Rachel managed to keep her tone even, although she resented the way Verdonia was dismissing them. She also found the explanation about Leo Erwin hard to believe. Mr. Venable had told her the two Templeton sisters were alone in the world, with no close relatives. Of course, Rachel had no way to discount Verdonia's explanation of the stranger's visit.

Ricky protested a little, but Verdonia cut that short by popping a bonbon into his open mouth, giving him a sharp slap on his bottom, a small push toward Rachel. Delphine had already retreated and slipped her hand into Rachel's.

Gladys, tight-lipped and red-faced, was waiting in the nursery to help the children with their baths and to serve them their supper. Rachel could tell she was upset. However, not wanting to discuss the unusual turn of events downstairs and Verdonia's flashy caller in front of the children, Rachel went to her room. If she had stayed she would not have trusted herself to refrain from questioning Gladys about what had happened in their absence. The more she thought about it, the flimsier Verdonia's explanation seemed. The cousin story seemed fabricated. Deeply troubled, Rachel decided to go talk to Mrs. Coulter.

There, however, instead of the calm counsel and comfort she sought, Rachel was confronted with an unexpected and dire situation.

At Rachel's knock, a flushed Mrs. Coulter opened the door. "Oh, come in, my dear," the housekeeper said breathlessly.

Rachel stepped into chaos. She looked around in utter bewilderment. The housekeeper's usually neat, cozy apartment was in total disarray. An open trunk stood in the middle of the floor, and it looked as though the housekeeper was packing for a trip. "What on earth are you doing?"

"What does it look like? I'm leaving!" Mrs. Coulter continued wrapping one of her dozen silver-framed photographs in tissue paper. "I should have left weeks ago. The minute that woman came, I knew it was trouble. But I had no idea it would come to this."

"Come to *what?* Please, Mrs. Coulter, please tell me what happened for you to take this drastic step?"

Her mouth working nervously, Mrs. Coulter took a few steps one way, then back the other, holding the tissue-covered picture in both hands. Then she stood still, tears filling faded blue eyes.

"Come, sit down. Tell me just what happened." Rachel led her to an armchair.

Mrs. Coulter sniffed. "I've never been treated like this in my entire life! I've always been treated with dignity and politeness. *Until* this afternoon." Mrs. Coulter took a lace-edged handkerchief out of her sleeve and wiped her eyes and her red nose. "*That* woman—she came to me this afternoon—after that, that *dreadful* fellow . . ." Mrs. Coulter's mouth twisted with disdain . . . "arrived!

"Did you ever see such a suit, such a tie, such shoes?" she demanded indignantly. "Her *cousin* she says! I'm sure Mrs. Sophia never had a relative like that." She sniffed. "Anyway, *she* came, pounding on my door and demanded—yes, *demanded*—my keys!" With a pudgy finger the housekeeper pointed to the ornamental ring, the chatelaine, now hanging empty on her belt.

"What she wanted was the key to the wine cellar. When I told her she would have to get that one from Melton, she practically accused me of lying, said with all the keys hanging on my ring there must be a duplicate to the wine cellar! I was so angry I handed her *all* the keys, told her if she didn't believe me she could try all of them."

Mrs. Coulter wagged her head until her silver curls, peeping out from the now askew lace cap, danced. "I won't say what she said to that. I'm too much of a lady to repeat such language. Then she grabbed my keys and flounced out of here."

The household keys! How reckless of Verdonia to bring on this crisis. The housekeeper's authority had been challenged.

The keys were the symbol of the trust the owners placed in her. Verdonia had stepped across the line.

"I would have left long before this, probably should have." Mrs. Coulter sighed. "It was only my loyalty to Mr. Venable and my affection for the children that has kept me here."

"Oh, please, Mrs. Coulter, do reconsider. We all depend on you so. I can't bear to think of your leaving." Rachel wondered what she would do if left alone at Talisman.

"My mind's made up, Rachel. I can't stay—not after this."

Rachel tried her best to calm her down, dissuade her. She got only a partial consent, a promise to do nothing until *she* had a chance to talk to Verdonia.

"I'm sure she regrets acting so hastily."

"It won't do any good, Rachel. She dislikes me, has from the very first, and I can't stand her. Oh, if dear Mrs. Sophia were only alive or Mr. Venable were here—but you must understand it's impossible for me to stay with that woman in charge."

"Please, Mrs. Coulter, if she apologizes?"

Mrs. Coulter would not answer, and Rachel left her room with a sinking heart. But she had to try to mend this breach. Verdonia was probably already having second thoughts about her impulsive action, one of her sudden irrational rages.

Although it was hardly the governess's place to intercede in this matter, Rachel knew Mrs. Coulter's leaving would be a disaster. There was nothing else to do but present that fact to Verdonia.

Rachel waited until the children were asleep and Verdonia's guest had been taken to the train station by a disgruntled Melton, then gathering all her courage she marched down the hall to discuss the incident with Verdonia.

Verdonia listened coldly to Rachel's plea that the housekeeper's ruffled feathers be smoothed and peace be restored.

"Surely, you're not suggesting I apologize to the old biddy?"

"Miss Templeton, Mrs. Coulter has been housekeeper here for many years and—"

"Maybe it's been too long, Miss Penniston. I don't take orders from servants. May I remind you I am in charge here now."

It took all Rachel's willpower not to respond. It was useless to continue. In Verdonia's present vindictive mood, any further argument might result in her own dismissal. Rachel could not risk that. For the children's sake. Personally, she would gladly have walked out and left the contentious place Talisman had become. But she could not leave the children with someone like Verdonia Templeton.

Disheartened, Rachel went back to Mrs. Coulter's room. Sadly, she watched Mrs. Coulter finish her packing, her determination to leave fortified by Rachel's report.

"Don't worry about me, Rachel. I shall not go long without another place. I have many opportunities. I've had offers of employment even since I came here to Talisman. I'll certainly not ask a reference from *her,* but I intend to write Mr. Venable and tell him frankly what led to my departure. You know, Rachel, he really should be told what's going on here. If he knew, I believe he'd come home straightaway." Mrs. Coulter's double chin jiggled indignantly.

The next day Rachel stood at the window in the housekeeper's deserted apartment, watching the carriage carrying Mrs. Coulter to the train station go down the drive. She felt alone and lost, as if the weight of the world had suddenly dropped onto her shoulders.

That night a terrifying storm broke. Loud thunder rattled Rachel awake. She heard Delphine's frightened call and jumped out of bed, ran into the little girl's room, picked her up in her arms, and soothed her. Ricky slept on undisturbed.

It wasn't only the outside storm that made Delphine sleep so lightly, it was also the storm within the house. As sensitive a child as Delphine was, she could not help but be aware of the turmoil in the house. Mrs. Coulter had bid the children an emotional good-bye, and though Ricky had seemed to take it in his stride, Delphine had wept and clung to the housekeeper.

Rachel knew Dede would not settle back to sleep easily, so she carried her back into her own bedroom, tucked her into the down comforter, and told her a favorite story until she fell asleep.

There were further rumbles of thunder, and frequently the sky lit up with jagged streaks of lightning. Rachel did not find it easy to go to sleep herself. She was sometimes able to be free of her worries and responsibilities in sleep, but now the weight of them seemed crushing. Sleep eluded her.

The next day when she asked Verdonia what they were to do about hiring another housekeeper, Verdonia looked at Rachel with feigned astonishment.

"Another housekeeper? Nonsense! I don't know just what Mrs. Coulter did anyhow. Very little, if you ask me. And paid an exorbitant annual wage, I suspect. Certainly we can manage without her."

Verdonia went back to her newspaper saying indifferently, "I know how to order food from the greengrocer and certainly what to tell the servants to do. What else is there?"

Bewildered, Rachel turned away. Verdonia thought she could run a house like the experienced Mrs. Coulter had done for many years. It would be quite a feat. But there was nothing she could do.

16

*I*f things had seemed to be gradually deteriorating at Talisman before Mrs. Coulter left, after her departure, things worsened daily. Melton did his best to keep things running smoothly. However, in large country homes such as Talisman, where specific responsibilities rarely overlapped, a butler had his assigned area of authority, the housekeeper hers. When one of these important positions remained unfilled, the whole household suffered.

With no one to direct special cleaning jobs, the maids became lax. Dust began to accumulate on surfaces that used to gleam, brasses once bright with polish tarnished. Floors and banisters were dull, windowpanes smudged. Fireplaces were not always cleaned nor fires laid regularly. Flowers were not replaced in vases every day. The entire house began to slide into disarray.

Rachel felt helpless to do anything. She had no say in the running of the household. It was enough for her to keep the children on an even keel, which Verdonia's on-again, off-again relationship with them constantly threw out of kilter. Sometimes Verdonia wanted them in her room, amusing her, fetching and carrying for her. Other days she slept until noon and did not want to be disturbed.

Much to Rachel's displeasure Leo became a frequent visitor. Rachel did not trust the man, and she deeply doubted he was related to Verdonia. Erwin's oily manner gave her shudders. He had a roving eye. He often tried to engage her in conversation. If they passed each other in the hall or stairway—something she tried to avoid—he was apt to make inappropriate comments on her appearance, her dress, or her bonnet. The children were often her shield against what otherwise might become unwelcome advances. Especially Delphine, who no longer wanted to be with her aunt, unless cajoled to do so.

Over and over Rachel wished Tony would come. But he did not. Rachel thought about him with both anger and longing. She needed to confide her fears, pour out her doubts. With Mrs. Coulter gone and Tony still out of the country, she had no one to whom she could turn. Tony's scrawled postcards from Paris in no way assuaged her anxiety, nor diminished her need to see him. She missed his confident presence.

One night, worried and sleepless, Rachel was standing at her bedroom window when she thought she saw someone moving out of the maze toward the house.

Frozen with fear, she held her breath in horror. The figure disappeared into the shadows. Rachel blinked. Had she really seen something, someone? Or was it her imagination? Was it possible someone was lurking around, observing the house, scouting for a way to gain entry?

A sudden rush of courage surged up in Rachel. She whirled around, ran out of the bedroom and down through the darkened house, frantically checking all the entrances.

She found nothing. Everything was locked, and there was no sign of tampering with door handles or latches. She started to return upstairs when she was halted once more by sounds. A low murmuring—voices, movement? Heart pounding, she strained to listen. It seemed to come from the back of the house, past the dining room, from the pantry or kitchen.

Inching along the dark hallway, Rachel put out a shaky hand, carefully pushed open the green baize door leading into the servants' hall and beyond it into the kitchen. The creak of its hinges must have alerted whoever it was; suddenly all was quiet. Eerily quiet. Except for Rachel's pounding heart, roaring loudly in her ears.

A dim light shone from under the crack of the kitchen door. Her mouth dry with fear, Rachel wanted to turn and run. It took all her determination not to, that having come this far she was going to find out whatever it was that lay behind the door. She boldly stepped into the kitchen and gasped.

Facing her was Melton, standing at the sink, a dishcloth in his hand. "Miss Penniston!" he greeted her with dignified surprise. "Is anything wrong? May I help you in some way?"

Rachel shook her head. "No, no I just thought—well, I heard something and came down to check."

"Sorry, miss, if you were alarmed. I am just having my usual cup of tea before retiring for the night."

Rachel knew it was not considered proper for a member of the household to invade the butler's domain, and she felt embarrassed to have done so. Her excuse seemed inadequate, an affront to Melton's position. His face was impassive, but Rachel saw rebuke in his eyes.

"Not at all, Melton," she stammered. "It is I who should apologize—" She turned to go, when her glance caught something. Melton was drying a cup, which he placed in its saucer on the drainboard. But there was another cup and saucer on the kitchen table. Who had been sharing a midnight snack with Melton? Butlers hardly ever deigned to socialize with the maids. Rachel's stomach contracted painfully.

Impeccable as Melton was he was human after all. He may have sought the companionship of Sue or Molly, the pretty house and parlor maids. However, it didn't seem likely. It was another possibility that disturbed Rachel a great deal more. Had Melton been entertaining an outsider? Someone who might be a threat? Trying to conceal her trembling, Rachel left, saying over her shoulder, "Good night, Melton."

"Good night, miss." His voice sounded odd, somehow intimidating. Upstairs, Rachel tried to rid herself of suspicion. Melton had been with the Venables since they first came here. Brett Venable trusted him.

Still the incident upset her. Sleep was difficult and long in coming.

Day by day some sense of foreboding grew stronger, pervading the entire household. Rachel's stomach seemed always knotted. She felt inadequate and ill-prepared to shoulder the responsibilities Mrs. Coulter's leaving had placed on her. Mr. Venable had assured her his loyal staff would carry on with their usual efficiency as though he were in residence. The thing that troubled Rachel was whether she could have done anything to alleviate the tension between Mrs. Coulter and Verdonia before it reached such a crisis. Had she been too distracted by her own feelings of resentment, jealousy, or even her attraction to Tony? Had she failed the trust Mr. Venable had placed in her?

Even though oppressed by doubts and uncertainties, Rachel felt a necessity to project calm, as if it was up to her to hold back some unknown disaster, perhaps even something sinister.

It was not long in coming. Certain valuable things, such as pieces of silver, fine porcelain figurines and vases, came up missing. Rachel's first awareness of this was when she overheard Melton questioning Molly about a pair of small Chinese vases and a cut-glass candy dish that had mysteriously disappeared.

"Now, tell the truth, lass. Are you sure you didn't break it and hide it so's not to be found out?"

"No, sir, Mr. Melton. It weren't me, sir. Cross my heart. I never broke nothing, took nothing." Molly's aggrieved voice dissolved into sobs. "I'm an honest person, Mr. Melton. I'd never do that."

"There, there, lass. Don't cry," Rachel heard Melton say awkwardly as she tiptoed past, not wanting to intrude.

It did not end there with that incident. Soon, several other things could not be found in their usual places, and in Mrs. Coulter's absence, a concerned Melton reported to Rachel. Rachel did not know what to do. She could not act on her own. Something had to be done. Mr. Venable's property had been stolen during his absence. Since Verdonia was temporarily head of the house, Rachel had no alternative but to tell her. So one morning right after Gladys had taken away Verdonia's breakfast tray, Rachel went into her sitting room and reported the thefts.

Verdonia's face contorted, flushed angrily. "Well! We'll put a stop to this right away! I've never trusted these servants. They're always lurking about, spying, watching for a chance, no doubt, to snatch something—I'll have none of it."

The next morning, Verdonia ordered all the servants to line up in the front hall and remain there while she personally searched their rooms on the third floor.

Rachel was appalled. Mr. Venable had vouched for his household staff. None had been with the family less than five years. Their faces reflected their shock and humiliation.

The unthinkable happened. Verdonia returned after her "investigative inspection" with a triumphant look on her face. She held up a pair of crystal bud vases. Then she pointed to Allan, the footman.

"And how do you explain these? Hidden in your footlocker under your bed?"

Red-faced, spluttering, Allan protested his innocence.

Verdonia shook her head, silencing him. "Dismissed. I want you off these premises. Right now."

Melton stepped forward, as if to defend the young footman. Again Verdonia would hear none of it. She speared him with a glare. "Enough. I have a duty to maintain my brother-in-law's home and property. Let this be a lesson to all of you." With that, she turned and swept up the stairs without looking back.

Rachel surveyed the stunned faces of the servants. A murmur went down the line, and Gladys, particularly, looked furious. Rachel recalled that Gladys and Allan were walking out together on their days off. For a minute her eyes met Rachel's, and Rachel was taken aback by the cold hostility in them. Did she somehow blame *her* for not speaking up in Allan's defense? Then Gladys followed the others out to the servants' hall.

Rachel could only imagine what discussion took place there.

During the following days, Rachel felt doubly disquieted. Not just because of the way the entire matter had been conducted by Verdonia, but also because she didn't believe Allan was the culprit. He had always appeared to be a forthright young man, and his denial seemed genuine. The other thing that disturbed her was Gladys's reaction. Just when Rachel had begun to feel Gladys's grudging acceptance, this had destroyed their budding friendship. One Rachel wanted and felt she needed.

Rachel debated whether there was anything she could do to get Allan reinstated. He had always seemed a cheerful sort, always willing to help or do an errand or extra chore. The children loved him. He always had a smile, a playful word for them. But Rachel realized she did not have personal proof of his honesty, and approaching Verdonia would just mean a heated, likely futile, confrontation. While she procrastinated, Rachel felt the repercussions of Allan's dismissal. The servants, shocked and resentful at his treatment, became silent and sullen. A feeling of impending doom hovered over the entire house, trapping everyone in a claustrophobic mood of suspicion.

Only a few days after that deplorable scene, Rachel met Gladys coming up the stairs. The maid neither smiled nor spoke. As she attempted to pass, Rachel caught her arm to halt her.

"Gladys—" Gladys tried to pull away, but Rachel tightened her hold. "Gladys, wait—please. Is it about Allan? Is that what's the matter?"

Gladys's eyes glittered with anger. "What's the matter, miss? Don't you know? You could've spoke up for Allan, and you didn't. You know good and well he never stole them vases, never took nuthin' that didn't belong to him."

"Then who, Gladys? They *were* found in his room—" Rachel faltered.

"Someone could've put them there. It weren't him, I know that much," Gladys declared stubbornly. Then as she started up the stairs again, she said over her shoulder, "You know wot they say—it takes a thief to catch a thief."

"Gladys—" Rachel tugged at her sleeve to make her stop. "I'm sorry, truly I am. Please don't be angry at me. Miss Templeton *is* after all in charge while Mr. Venable is gone. What could I do? I have to stay with the children; I can't take the chance she might dismiss *me,* then what would happen to Dede and Ricky?"

Rachel saw she had hit a nerve with Gladys. She lowered her voice. "Gladys, we have to protect the children. I need you to help me. And if Allan isn't guilty then we'll both try to find out *who* the thief *is*—together."

Gladys pursed her mouth, as if considering what Rachel said. She sighed and nodded. "I spose you're right, miss. I shouldn't blame *you.* But we better keep our eyes and ears open. There's sumpin strange goin' on here."

Rachel hoped she had convinced Gladys she intended to get to the bottom of the thefts. Rachel wasn't sure *how,* but she was going to try, and she needed Gladys's support. Rachel pondered Gladys's remark, "You know wot they say—it takes a thief to catch a thief."

Rachel was more sure than ever Allan hadn't stolen the vases. Something very strange *was* going on at Talisman, and she meant to get to the bottom of it.

17

The children reflected the undercurrent of tension in the household. Rachel tried to protect them from the ill will among the adults by planning special excursions, games, and stories to keep them distracted. Because Leo Erwin came more and more often, they were excluded from their aunt's company. Sounds of laughter, voices, and the clink of wine glasses could be heard from behind the closed door of the drawing room where Verdonia entertained him.

Then something happened to increase Rachel's suspicion and her growing conviction that something devious was going on at Talisman.

One evening when Rachel and the children were in her sitting room, the children decided they wanted to hear a story other than the one Rachel had planned to read to them. Rachel sent Delphine down the hall to the schoolroom to fetch the other book. The little girl had been gone only a few minutes when Rachel heard her cry out.

"What are you doing with Mama's bird?"

"You little sneak, what were you doing spying on me?" came Verdonia's shrill voice.

Rachel rushed to the door and out into the hall, Ricky on her heels. She saw Delphine, looking terrified, pressed against the wall. Verdonia was just getting to her feet from crouching on the floor in front of the cabinet where Sophia's Lalique collection was displayed. The doors stood open. Verdonia, face flushed, stared at Delphine, shaking her fist at the child. In her other hand she clutched the small, winged, crystal bird.

"What's going on?" Rachel gasped.

Delphine cast a frightened look at Rachel, one that said *rescue me.* Tears rolled down her cheeks.

Verdonia stooped to pick up the ring of household keys taken from Mrs. Coulter. They had dropped to the floor.

Verdonia then turned on Rachel. "I suggest you tend to your duties, Miss Penniston. The children should be in bed by this time, not roaming around the halls looking for mischief."

"But what happened?"

Delphine sidled over toward Rachel, and Rachel held out her hand.

"If you *must* know, this valuable collection belonged to my sister and I was checking to see if any pieces were missing. After all the thefts that have happened—" She stopped, seeming flustered, then hurriedly went on, "We may have a thief in this house, Miss Penniston, and I intend to find out who it is."

Rachel started to ask if she now thought her accusation of Allan had been wrong, but she refrained. She had a frightened little girl on her hands. Dede was clinging to her skirt, trembling. Rachel had to control her own anger. She reminded herself the children were her most important concern. This was not the time for another confrontation with their aunt.

Verdonia seemed to attempt a conciliatory tone as she said, "I'm sorry I yelled at you like that, Dede. You startled me, creeping up on me like that." She smiled. "Can you forgive auntie?"

The smile seemed forced, the sweetness false. But the little girl nodded slowly.

"Well, then, run along with Miss Penniston. Don't worry, auntie isn't cross with you." Then Verdonia's voice changed again, becoming firm. "I intend to make an inventory of this collection, and if any of the pieces are missing it will confirm my suspicions of theft. I also intend to interrogate the servants and find the culprit. Perhaps the servants think because their master is away they can get away with something like this. I shall show them they cannot."

Rachel and the two subdued children returned to her sitting room. It was all she could do to keep her own composure, to get through the story, and to get them settled for the night. Whimpering, Dede asked if she could sleep in Rachel's bed. Rachel gently told her no, but she sat with them both until they fell asleep.

By the time she got back to her own bedroom Rachel was exhausted, emotionally drained. She longed to have one full night of unbroken sleep, but her mind was in a turmoil. What was *really* going on?

A recurring thought had deeply troubled Rachel. Could the blow on the head Verdonia received in the train wreck have transformed her character to such an extreme extent that she—? No, it couldn't be.

Yet, Rachel's distrust of Verdonia had grown steadily.

Rachel struggled with her dislike of Verdonia Templeton. Was she judging too harshly a woman who could be seriously impaired? If only Tony were here, her longing heart cried. His postcards had become fewer and farther apart. Each one that came now made her resentful instead of giving her delight. She imagined he was having an enjoyable time, attending embassy parties, fetes, and balls, being flirtatiously flattered by dark-eyed beauties. She was here by herself, surrounded by mysterious and threatening forces.

Over and over she considered writing to Brett Venable. Now that Mrs. Coulter was no longer here, sending him weekly reports, should Rachel take that up as her duty? But what would she say? *Dear Sir, your sister-in-law is causing grave discord and disruption in your home—* While she debated what course to take, things grew steadily worse.

Rachel had nightmares that all the servants would leave, that she would wake up some morning and find the house empty—empty of all but her and Verdonia. It was becoming increasingly hard for her to sleep at night. She lay long awake, listening for something, waiting for something. Something she dreaded but instinctively *knew* was coming. Something that would finally clarify things. The house seemed filled with weird sounds, stealthy footsteps, and whisperings.

Then came the night she *knew* she had heard something. It was no mistake. She sat up in bed. She got up, flung on her robe, armed herself with the fireplace poker, and tiptoed out to the hall and to the children's bedroom. Having satisfied herself they were both sleeping safely, she proceeded to the top of the staircase, then to the landing. She stood there for a long moment, listening. In spite of her fear, she forced herself on, creeping down step by step, until she reached the bottom. Heart pumping, she slipped across the hall, past the drawing room, then paused outside the closed dining room doors. Here, her breath coming fast, she stopped short.

Someone was in there, she was sure. She heard movement, rustling, the plink of metal. With a shaky hand, she reached out and quietly turned the handle of the door, pushed the door open slightly, peered through the crack. The shadowy outline of a person was silhouetted against the wavering light from an oil lamp set upon the massive mahogany sideboard. A man's figure, hunched forward, emptying the silverware drawers into a large bag.

Outrage overcame any thought of danger. "Stay right where you are. I have a weapon!"

With a clatter of dropping silver, the man spun around, and Rachel saw his startled face. *Melton!* Her grip on the raised poker loosened, and her arm fell to her side. "Melton!"

"Miss Penniston," he gasped raggedly.

Stunned, she stared at him.

"Oh, miss, it's not what it looks like, what you might think. I can explain," he sputtered. "I've been very concerned—worried—as you must be, too, miss, about the disappearance of valuables, every day something coming up missing. I never believed Allan to be guilty, but someone is. There's a thief in this house, miss, that I'm sure of. So what I was doin' here, miss, I thought to take the silver to my own room for safekeeping, just bring it out as need be each day . . ." His voice trailed away weakly, as if he himself was conscious of how threadbare his excuse really was.

"Do you really think that's necessary, Melton?" Rachel asked, knowing she was treading on dangerous ground to question the man's integrity. Melton had been with the Venable family for years. Why would he begin to steal from them *now?* Though his guilty manner and failure to meet her direct gaze troubled Rachel, she wanted to believe Melton was telling the truth, as transparent as his excuse seemed.

"Well, I know Mr. Venable trusts your judgment implicitly. He told me I could rely on you absolutely. That's what I want to do." She hesitated. "I'm relieved it was you I heard. I thought it might be a burglar." Again she halted. There seemed nothing more to say. "So I'll say good night."

"Good night, miss."

Still feeling unsettled and suspicious, Rachel climbed the stairs and went back to her room. It wasn't until she was back in bed, trying to go to sleep, that she remembered the night she had found Melton in the kitchen and seen the extra teacup. Did Melton have a partner? Someone who came by dark and took away the stolen goods Melton collected? She didn't want to think of Melton as a thief, but what else could she think? Who else could it be?

Rachel felt trapped in the deepening dilemma at Talisman. Verdonia's irrational behavior, her own suspicions of Melton, and vague, unnamed fears increased every day.

Leo Erwin was more and more making himself at home at Talisman, he and Verdonia closeted behind the closed doors of her suite for longer and longer periods of time.

Rachel had all kinds of suspicions about Verdonia. She particularly suspected the association with Leo Erwin. Her dislike of him strengthened with every encounter. He seemed such a sleazy character for Verdonia to *know*, much less be related to. Round and round Rachel went, reviewing the strange things that had happened since Verdonia's arrival. Talisman was not at all the place it had been when Rachel came. Everything had changed.

Her own position precarious, Rachel was the only protection the children had. Delphine had completely turned away from her aunt and stayed close to Rachel. Although Ricky was still in favor, Rachel was very worried about him. From a sunny, carefree child, he had become a troubled and unhappy little boy.

It all came to a head one day when Rachel inadvertently came upon a distressing scene. Returning from another of her uneasy days off, Rachel was crossing the lawn toward the terrace when she saw Leo Erwin bending over Ricky, the little boy's arm caught behind him in the man's grip.

In a nasty tone of voice Leo said, "How'd you like it if I kidnapped you? Sold you to pirates, huh? They'd make you walk the plank, and you'd get eaten by crocodiles. How'd you like *that?*"

Rachel rushed up the terrace steps. "What do you think you're doing?" she demanded of a suddenly red-faced Erwin. He dropped Ricky's arm and gave a forced chuckle. Ricky threw himself at Rachel, his arms circling her, holding tight.

"How dare you frighten a little boy like that?" Rachel asked furiously.

Leo adjusted his cravat somewhat uncomfortably, gave Rachel a broad wink. "Ah, come on. I wuz jest playin' with the lad. Weren't I, old fellow?" With that he leaned forward and tweaked Ricky's ear.

Rachel felt the boy's whole body quiver.

"From now on, Mr. Erwin, I'll thank you to leave this child alone," Rachel said icily. She put her arm protectively around Ricky's shoulder and led him away.

This was too much. *This* could go no further. She would tell Verdonia in no uncertain terms that Leo Erwin was not a fit person to be around the children. Surely, as their aunt, she would understand Rachel's indignation when she related this incident.

But Verdonia passed the whole incident off as nothing. "Leo's a tease. He enjoys playing with the children. Spoofing was what he was doing. Nothing else." She gave Rachel a withering look. *"Again,* Miss Penniston, you're making a mountain out of a molehill. I think the *real* trouble is you! You're overprotective of the children. You're making them timid whiners, tattletales!"

Rachel could hardly contain herself. "The children are *my* charge, Miss Templeton. Anything I deem harmful to them is within my responsibility to address. I think Mr. Erwin's behavior was inappropriate. Ricky was really frightened."

Verdonia's expression hardened. "It is my opinion, Miss Penniston, that you have overstepped your authority. I think *you* are the one at fault. I believe the children would be better off without your kind of *protection."* She paused then said maliciously, "If I hear another one of your groundless complaints, you can consider yourself given notice. Do I make myself clear?"

Cold fury coursed through Rachel. She drew herself up, and staring straight at Verdonia said evenly, "You can't fire me, Miss Templeton. *Mr. Venable* hired me. I have a signed contract and I am to stay here with the children until his return. You have no authority to break that agreement."

Verdonia paled, then flushed crimson. Her mouth twisted, then drew into a straight line.

"We'll just see about that, Miss Penniston," was all she managed to say, but her hands clenched until the knuckles were white.

Holding herself very straight, Rachel left the room. As she closed the door of Verdonia's room, she slumped slightly against it, her knees suddenly weak. For a few seconds, marveling that she had really stood up to Verdonia like that, she closed her eyes. When she opened them, she found Gladys standing down the hall a short distance away, a look of surprised admiration on her face.

After that Verdonia dropped any pretense of civility toward Rachel. She treated her like a piece of furniture, ignoring her, avoiding contact. When she had to address her, it was with disdain.

The unexpected bonus of this confrontation was that Gladys's attitude toward her thawed. On Rachel's next day off, Gladys made a point to assure her she would be with the children all afternoon, that Rachel was not to worry.

*R*achel welcomed some time to herself. Her nerves had been wound up tight, especially since her open confrontation with Verdonia. On duty, Rachel was always tensely aware of her responsibilities, never relaxed. Today with the children safely in Gladys's care she was determined to enjoy her free afternoon.

There was a tinge of early autumn in the air, and the walk to the village was invigorating. Fall had always been Rachel's favorite time of year, although it meant the days were shorter, that evening came on sooner and darkness fell quickly.

She window-shopped along the main street before going into the bookstore. As she entered, she noticed a display of travel books on a table near the door and stopped to browse. How wonderful it would be to travel. She picked up a beautiful book about Italy and looked at pictures of Italian hillsides, Venetian gondoliers, paintings at the Uffizi museum in Florence. Then she selected a book entitled *Paris*. It was filled with scenes of chestnut trees in bloom, the Luxembourg Gardens, the Bois, houseboats on the Seine. How romantic it would be to stroll along the boulevards, see all this. Paris. Tony's last postcard had been of a picturesque sidewalk cafe. Longing vied with resentment. He was probably seeing some of these lovely places right now. Turning the pages slowly, Rachel was tempted to buy the book, but at length she put it down. It would just rub salt in the wound. Missing him more when he was far away and probably not giving her a thought.

Just then she happened to look up and see through the store window the tall figure of a man passing by outside. It was Ross Sinclair, the railroad company inspector. What was he doing in Craigburne? Surely there hadn't been that many victims of the train wreck in this small village to warrant a continued investigation. Rachel remembered that the day she herself arrived only two or three other passengers had gotten off at the station with her.

In the light of all that had happened since he'd brought Verdonia's belongings, Rachel had some questions of her own. Impulsively, she hurried out of the store to follow him. But when she came outside, he was nowhere to be seen. She went in the direction he had been walking, but he seemed to have disappeared.

Seeing him again had brought a dozen questions into Rachel's mind, which churned with all the scattered bits and pieces of disconcerting events at Talisman.

She walked a little farther down the street, then turned and retraced her steps. In such a small town, how could he have vanished so quickly? Finally frustrated, she mentally shook herself. She had hoped to enjoy this day off for a change. The children were safe with Gladys, and *she* should try to forget her worries for a few hours.

Determinedly Rachel went into the small milliner's shop and spent a pleasurable half an hour trying on bonnets. She ended up buying one she couldn't afford because she felt guilty for taking up so much of the clerk's time. Adding to her extravagance, she went to the Harbor Inn and ordered herself a large pot of tea and a slice of poppy seed cake.

By the time she finished, it was after four o'clock. The wind off the ocean was strong and cold as she hurried along the esplanade and turned onto the inland country road.

She should have left sooner, she told herself. It would be almost dark before she reached Talisman. The autumn dusk was falling quickly.

Rachel wasn't quite sure when it began. At first it was simply a prickly, oddly unpleasant, sensation. Then she felt a chilling certainty she was being followed. She halted, listening. The footsteps she'd thought she heard stopped also. Fear rippled through her. Her mouth went dry and her heart thumped wildly.

She started walking again, fear quickening her pace. Every nerve tingled. Perspiration beaded her forehead, her upper lip. She dared not stop again or turn around to see if anyone was really following. Telling herself not to panic, she took longer steps, her heart and pulse racing, the sensation she was being followed strong.

Ahead of her loomed the peaked outline of Talisman's roof. She still had to get to the gates and go through the maze to reach the house.

Breathless, she pushed through the gate. Entering the maze, she heard a footstep crunch on the gravel path behind her. She whirled around and thought she saw a shadowy figure a few paces behind her. Her heart clutched. She lifted her skirt and began to run.

There was a jabbing pain in her side, and her legs felt weak as she stumbled and almost fell. Sure now whoever was following her was close, she ducked into one of the turns of the tall boxwood hedge, shrank back against it, trembling. If her pursuer came by, she would stick out her foot, trip him, then take advantage of his fall and run for the house.

Her breath shallow, she waited. Suddenly she felt movement behind her. Before she could turn around or make a sound, a hand clapped itself over her mouth. She struggled to get away. A strangled scream lodged in her throat. The hand pressed harder. Her fingers pried at the hand on her mouth.

Then she heard a voice in her ear, "Don't scream, Rachel. It's Tony!" His grip gradually loosened.

She whirled around, and in the growing darkness, she saw it *was* Tony. "Tony!"

"I'm sorry if I hurt you, Rachel. I didn't want to. It's just that I couldn't let you see me until I was sure *we* wouldn't be seen—especially from the house."

All Rachel could do was stare at him. Weak with relief, all she could say was, "You frightened me half to death. I thought you were in France!"

"I was. I mean, that's what I wanted everyone to believe."

"But the postcards?"

"I wrote them, sent them to a friend in Paris to remail them so the postmarks would be right."

"But why? I don't understand."

"I thought it was safer for you to believe I was out of the country."

"Safer? What do you mean? Why all the silly games when I needed you?" Rachel had forgotten she had decided not to ever tell him she missed him or cared.

"I'll explain everything later. But now, listen to me carefully, Rachel. We don't have much time. You're probably expected back at the house right now. I've found out some things—serious things—some evidence—"

Rachel cut him off. "Evidence? Oh, Tony, if you only knew what's been going on."

"I do know. Some of it anyway. That's what I have to tell you, Rachel. I'm here. Staying at Talisman."

"You're *what?"*

"Melton knows. I'm staying in the servants' quarters."

"You were Melton's mysterious midnight visitor?"

"I'm afraid so."

"What are you doing here?"

"I'm protecting my brother's children, I hope. I'm gathering information about Verdonia."

"Verdonia?"

"Or whoever she is."

"What do you mean?"

"I suspect that Verdonia, or rather the woman who *says* she's Verdonia Templeton, *isn't.*"

Stunned, Rachel asked, "How do you know?"

"Right from the first, certain things didn't ring true about her. I couldn't put my finger on it exactly. Except her accent. It's a London accent, not Canadian. Although I'm not sure what a Canadian one sounds like. But there were other things that bothered me. I thought I remembered Verdonia was *left-*handed, yet *she* uses her *right* hand. I watched her pour lemonade and when we played croquet—well—" He broke off.

"And?" Rachel prompted. "What else?"

"Then there were her earrings."

"Earrings?"

"I mean she wasn't wearing them. Neither were they in the jewel box the inspector brought. You see, when I first met Verdonia she was wearing ornate fire opal earrings. They were noticeable, dangling sort of, when she moved her head, turned or anything. I remember them because she made a great point of telling me her father had given them to her for her twenty-first birthday. Evidently they were stones from a mine he owned in Australia and meant a great deal to her. I never saw her without them."

"But, Tony, what is it you suspect?"

"Rachel, I can't tell you everything now. I just wanted you to know I'm here."

Rachel wanted to ask more, but Tony rushed on. "I'll be back and forth. I've been in touch with Inspector Sinclair, who had his own suspicions."

He paused. "What really worries us—" He stopped again, as if debating whether to continue. "If this woman *is* an impostor, where is the *real* Verdonia Templeton? Inspector Sinclair says there are still people unaccounted for, bodies unclaimed. Did this woman murder her?"

Rachel stifled an exclamation.

"I'm sorry, Rachel. I don't mean to frighten you, but I feel I have to warn you. She may be dangerous, as well as that man who's been coming to see her. Inspector Sinclair is checking records on *him*. They may be in this together.

"Be careful, Rachel. Take care of the children, and don't take any chances. As soon as we have proof, we can act."

Rachel shivered violently, and Tony pulled her against him, held her tight, murmuring something she couldn't quite hear because her ear was pressed against his coat.

Then he released her. "You better go now."

"When will I see you again? How can I tell you if I discover anything?"

"Melton will let you know where and when."

Then Tony kissed her so thoroughly Rachel almost forgot the perilous situation in which they were involved.

"Go on in now," Tony said huskily as he turned her toward the house. "And remember, Rachel, be careful. If she suspects we are onto her—well, just be careful."

Tony's warning ringing in her mind, Rachel walked the rest of the way to the house she had desperately raced to reach. It no longer meant safety. Something dark dwelled there—something frightening—something evil.

Something that had come with Verdonia Templeton.

19

When Rachel came into the house, Gladys was waiting for her at the top of the stairs. "You're late, miss." She put her head to one side, gave Rachel a searching glance. "You look— Is anything wrong?"

It would have been a relief to share her new information with Gladys. Rachel knew she would be willing to help gather evidence. But Tony had impressed upon Rachel the importance of secrecy. No one else must know he was there. She had to keep her word.

"Just tired."

"Well, I've *really* got somethin' to tell you, miss."

Rachel regarded her warily. She had enough worries on her mind without hearing more complaints. However, from Gladys's expression, Rachel realized it was something she'd better hear.

"It's about Miss Verdonia, miss."

Of course, it would be. "I was afraid of that. What has she done now?"

"It ain't what she's done, miss. It's what she ain't done."

"What is that?"

"We better go into your room, miss." Gladys gave a furtive look over her shoulder.

"Very well." Mystified, Rachel led the way down the hall into her sitting room.

The minute she closed the door Gladys said, "It's these, miss." Gladys reached into her apron pockets and brought out a pile of envelopes and held them out to Rachel.

Puzzled, Rachel took them and fanned them out. They were business size envelopes, all addressed to Miss Verdonia Templeton in care of Talisman, Craigburne. The names of various banks, businesses, and legal firms were printed on the upper left hand corner, and all bore Canadian postmarks. The letters had been opened and looked somewhat wrinkled. As if they'd been crumpled.

Rachel looked to Gladys for some clue. After Mrs. Coulter's departure, Rachel had taken over the duty of sorting the mail every day. She went through it to pick out the letters Mr. Venable wrote regularly to the children. Rachel remembered seeing several of this type of envelope addressed to Verdonia since her arrival. It was the kind of correspondence one would expect her to receive as the head of her family's business.

Rachel frowned. "I don't understand. I always give Melton Miss Templeton's mail to be placed on her breakfast tray for you to take up to her."

"That's just it, miss. I do. Every day." Gladys drew herself up importantly. "What's queer is, I sometimes find them letters in her trash basket! Or stuffed into the bottom of the armoire. Isn't that a strange way to handle letters, miss?"

"But why in the world would she do that? These all look like business letters. Probably important. Some not even opened?" Rachel looked at Gladys.

Gladys gave a helpless shrug. "If you ask *me*, miss, she don't know what to do with them." She hesitated. "I've been wonderin' for quite a spell—considerin' 'er strange ways and all, the way she flies into a temper, blows hot and cold, if you'll excuse me sayin' so—I been wonderin' if mebbe—"

Gladys stopped, then tapping her forehead with her index finger said, "She still ain't—after the accident and all—not quite right in her head?"

That same thought had occurred to Rachel. She had dismissed it as too unlikely. Now as Gladys presented it, it seemed possible. Maybe Rachel had been harshly judging a woman who could not help herself. They had been warned by the doctors she might not be quite herself.

But how did that fit in with Tony's suspicions? It was all such a muddle. Could a concussion change a person's handedness from left to right? Could it be the explanation for everything? For Verdonia's bizarre behavior? And what about Leo Erwin? There were so many factors here that needed explaining.

Rachel felt Gladys's gaze upon her. Again, she was tempted to confide in her. Better not. Not until she'd done some investigating of her own.

"Thank you, Gladys, for bringing this to my attention." She tapped the edge of the envelopes on the palm of her hand. "I'll ask Miss Templeton about this."

"Yes, miss." Gladys looked skeptical.

After Gladys left, Rachel paced, debating what she should do. Maybe the accident *did* account for Verdonia's mood swings, her flashes of temper, erratic behavior. Unless what Tony suspected was true. That *this* Verdonia was not the real one.

Mr. Venable had implied the Templetons had vast holdings in Canada—mines, timber, and other investments. If these were communications pertaining to the family businesses, as they seemed to be, they were being neglected. The more Rachel thought about it, she recalled Verdonia had not received any personal letters. Nor had she put out any mail of her own to be posted. Something was terribly wrong here.

Feeling guilty, but convincing herself it was the necessary gathering of evidence Tony had discussed, Rachel went through the batch of letters. Some contained contracts needing Verdonia's signature. Some complained they had not received necessary authorizations or responses to conduct pending transactions. The most recent letters urged prompt replies and signatures.

Why would the *legitimate* recipient of these letters not answer them? Not respond to the legal demands, not sign previously agreed-to contracts?

This was not the *real* Verdonia Templeton.

As she stood clutching the letters in her hands, Rachel knew it was up to her to prove it.

O nce Rachel decided what she must do, she waited for the right time to search Verdonia's rooms. There she might discover the evidence Tony needed.

It was all so frightening. The dislike and distrust Rachel had felt all along might have a valid basis. That was somewhat reassuring. Still the thought of invading someone's privacy, as she intended doing, disturbed Rachel. Under most circumstances it would be an awful thing to do.

"Take care of the children," was one of the last things Tony had said to her. She must keep in mind her first responsibility was to protect them. If their real aunt had somehow been injured or, God forbid, *murdered,* and someone evil was taking her place, it was Rachel's duty to rip away the mask and expose her.

There was no option. She *had* to search Verdonia's rooms.

Unexpectedly, the following afternoon after Leo Erwin arrived, Verdonia ordered the barouche brought around, and they took off together. Rachel seized her chance.

She slipped into Verdonia's suite and closed the door quietly behind her. She moved cautiously into the middle of the room. A cloyingly sweet smell hung in the air. She recognized it as the exotic scent Verdonia used. Rachel looked around. On the dressing table, she saw the top had been carelessly left off the perfume bottle.

Rachel did not know exactly how to begin. Or where. She had never done anything like this before. The bureau was perhaps the place to start. She started with the two top drawers. She tried not to disturb things as she pushed aside piles of scarves, stockings, handkerchiefs. She looked under camisoles, petticoats, corset covers, but found nothing incriminating. She replaced everything carefully.

Not knowing just what she was looking for made it more difficult. She would probably know it when she saw it, if it was anything that would verify Tony's suspicions.

She looked in the armoire where Gladys had discovered some of the envelopes crammed behind Verdonia's shoes. But there was nothing there. Getting more anxious by the minute, Rachel stepped back and shut the doors. She glanced around.

The dressing table was the next place to look. One by one, she pulled out the drawers. One was cluttered with hairpins, cuticle scissors, some tangled ribbons, odds and ends. Another held Verdonia's cosmetics, powder, rouge, a bottle of henna, and assorted brushes.

In the lowest drawer she found the alligator jewelry case. Rachel had already seen its contents when it was opened the day Inspector Sinclair had brought it for identification. The small velvet bag that had contained the pearls was empty. Verdonia must be wearing them today. A quick check of the box ascertained there was no secret compartment where something could be concealed. There was no sign of the opal earrings Tony had mentioned.

Frustrated, Rachel shut the drawers. Her gaze again circled the room. If she only knew *what* she was searching for, it would be easier.

Then her glance rested on the graceful Louis XVI inlaid escritoire in the windowed alcove. A desk might be the logical place to look for correspondence or unanswered mail. Rachel crossed the room. Her hands shook as she opened drawers, peeked into pigeonholes. Nothing. In her haste, she knocked over the crystal inkwell. To her horror, black ink spilled, soaking into the blotter. She grabbed it up in one hand and reached with her other hand for a handkerchief from her pocket. Hastily, she wiped the wood surface so it wouldn't stain. The leather encased blotter slid to one side. Underneath were loose sheets of paper. Rachel's gaze fixed on line after line of handwriting. Over and over one name was written. Verdonia Templeton.

Why in the world was Verdonia inscribing her name dozens of times? Slowly comprehension came. The slant of the writing varied. It ranged from neat to barely legible. The loops and swirls, the shape of the letters changed. It was someone practicing a script. Copying a signature?

A flash of insight hit Rachel. Tony had mentioned the Verdonia he recalled was *left*-handed. Rachel examined the pages again. A *right*-handed person trying to match a *left*-handed person's signature. Of course, left-handed people held pens at a different angle. It would be very difficult to imitate that. But *that's* what Verdonia was trying to do.

Rachel corrected herself. That is what this *impostor* was trying to do. Then Rachel recalled that in several of the letters the request for Verdonia's signature had been repeated. Rachel recalled seeing in some of the more recently dated ones, "Your signature is urgently needed to be validated before any monies can be forwarded to you from our London bank."

Rachel felt weak, her knees buckled, and she had to sit down. She held the sheets of paper in trembling hands. With each successive sheet, the signature was getting more expert. The woman must have found some authentic examples of Verdonia Templeton's script and studiously copied it until she had it almost right. She could then sign the vouchers so that the Canadian banks would verify them to banks in London, who in turn would honor them and send the money to her here.

Was this the evidence Tony and Inspector Sinclair needed? How many of these pages could she take without them being missed? While she was trying to decide, the door burst open. Startled, Rachel jerked around, heart pounding, the sheets of paper slipping out of her hands and scattering across the rug.

A terrified Gladys stood in the doorway.

"Miss, miss, hurry. Get out of here. *Quick!* They're comin' back!"

Rachel scrambled to her feet, gathered up the papers off the floor, shuffled them into a semblance of order, shoved them back under the desk blotter.

Gladys stood, her body half-turned at the door, keeping a frantic lookout toward the stairway. "Do hurry, miss!" she whispered.

Rachel gave a final glance around the room to see if she had left any telltale signs of her search. Then, still clenching the sodden blotter and two sheets of practiced signatures, she dashed by Gladys and down the hall to her own room. As she passed the stair landing she heard Verdonia's high-pitched laugh, followed by Erwin's raucous one, as they came in the front door.

Not until she was safely behind her own closed door and she opened her ink-stained hand did Rachel realize Gladys must have seen her go into Verdonia's suite and stood guard for her all that time. Perhaps she should tell Gladys what Tony suspected.

Before she could make up her mind, a rapid knock on her door brought Rachel back to the moment. She opened it and found Molly, the parlor maid, flushed and frenzied.

"Oh, miss, I can't find Master Ricky. I went to bring him and Miss Dede in for their tea, but he's missing. I'm ever so afraid."

"Come, Molly. He's got to be somewhere on the property. We'll find him. He's probably playing some kind of trick on us. You know how mischievous he can be."

"He was out on the terrace with Miss Verdonia and her caller the last time I seen him. I thought mebbe they had taken him with them when they left again."

"Left again?" A cold fear crept over Rachel. Her heart plummeted. All her worst suspicions about Verdonia and that awful Leo rushed upon her. She thought of the vicious way Leo had tormented the little boy. What if somehow—

"Yes, miss. Miss Verdonia said it was cooler than she thought and she came back for her shawl. Master Ricky weren't with them. But when I went out to the terrace, Miss Dede was playing with her dolls and Master Ricky was nowhere around. Both of us have been lookin' and callin' but . . ." Molly's voice trailed off shakily.

Rachel ran down the stairs. A tearful Delphine was standing at the bottom. "Come on, Dede. Help me look for your brother," Rachel said. "He must be somewhere. We'll find him."

The afternoon sun already cast purple shadows on the lawn and gardens, making the maze appear dark and threatening. Taking the little girl's hand, Rachel hurried across the terrace, down the stone steps.

"He could be hiding, Rachel. You know how he likes to tease."

"You're right. Let's call him," Rachel suggested.

Entering the maze, Rachel recalled vividly the last time she had come through it, how frightened she had been. Rachel had never really liked the maze and usually avoided it. But it was one of the children's favorite places to play, and she tried to hide her own aversion when they were with her.

Now calling loudly, "Ricky, Ricky!" she and Dede started into the winding labyrinth. Delphine was not the least bit afraid and ran ahead of Rachel, disappearing even as Rachel moved more slowly into the maze.

"Now, Ricky, don't be naughty! Answer me!" Rachel raised her voice. She halted, straining for some indication he might be hiding nearby—smothered giggles maybe. Taking another turn into the maze she called again. "Please, Ricky. It's Rachel!"

"Ricky!" she cried, squatting down beside where he was hunched into a ball, his head on his knees, his body shaking. Rachel pulled him into her arms, and hugged him.

"What is it, Ricky? What happened?" she asked as she rocked him close.

"Cousin Leo—he said he was going to sell me to pirates! They'd cut my throat and make me walk the plank, and the crocodiles would eat me up!" He burst into choking sobs.

Rachel held him tight. "Nothing of the kind. That was wicked of him to tell you that. It's not true. No one is going to sell you or hurt you. Really and truly. I promise." She squeezed him reassuringly. "Come on, we'll go inside. You can have a nice, warm bath and supper. Everything will be all right. You don't need to be frightened anymore."

She took his clammy little hands in her own, pulled him to his feet. Together they started out of the maze. Just then they heard a piercing scream, Dede's voice calling "Rachel! Rachel!"

Rachel stopped. "Dede. What is it? I've found Ricky. Where are you?"

The high, thick hedge walls enclosed them, yet Dede's voice had sounded quite near where they were standing.

"Rachel, you must come see what I've found." The little girl's voice sounded shrill.

"I'm coming." Rachel gently pulled Ricky along with her and made several twisting turns through the maze before she came upon Dede, bending over something that looked like a burlap sack.

"Look, Rachel! I nearly tripped over this. It was sticking out from under this bush." She dragged the bag farther out into the path and tugged at the loosely tied knot that closed it. She put her hand inside and drew out a shoe box.

"There's something heavy inside, Rachel. Shall I open it?"

"Of course, open it!" Ricky said before Rachel could speak.

Delphine took the lid off, put her hand inside, and brought out a small object wrapped in paper. She looked up. Her face underwent a complete change. Her mouth opened and her eyes widened. "I think I know what's in here. I can feel the shape," she said in a hushed voice. "Rachel, it's—" She pulled aside the paper then held out her palm. A tiny crystal bird rested on it. "It's Mama's Lalique collection!"

Rachel gasped. She dropped Ricky's hand, and they all bent over to see what else was in the box. At least six of the delicate glass animal and bird figurines were inside.

"Someone put them here to steal them!" Delphine was indignant.

Out of the mouths of babes. This was no impulsive act of a servant ignorant of their immense value. Allan, the accused—no, the wrongly accused footman had been gone for weeks. No one could blame *him* this time. Rachel thought of the other missing items that no one had been able to find. The small but priceless things—teacups, bud vases, little porcelain figurines. Had they all been systematically stolen, one by one, bagged and placed out here in the maze for an accomplice to pick up?

A cold certainty formed within Rachel. Leo Erwin. Cruel, sadistic, amoral. A thief. Then Rachel remembered the night she and Delphine had come upon Verdonia at the glass cabinet containing the Lalique collection. No one else had the keys. They were both in this. Rachel didn't know *who* the woman posing as Verdonia Templeton was. However, Rachel was *sure* she was an intruder.

Immediately, Rachel came to a decision. She must get this information to Tony at once. Surely this would be enough evidence to confront the woman and her partner. Remembering the warning to be careful, Rachel knew she must not endanger the children. This would have to be handled with great care.

"Come on, children. We'll take these back inside. But you're not to say a word to anyone about our finding all this, all right?"

Both nodded solemnly.

On the lawn they met an anxious Gladys, who had just been told by Molly about Ricky's being missing.

"Thank goodness!" she exclaimed when she saw him. "And aren't you the dirty one! It's a bath for you right away. Playin' tricks again, I wager."

"Don't scold him, Gladys," Rachel interjected. "He's had a fright. I'll tell you about it later. Right now, we need your help."

Gladys's eyes popped wide at Rachel's whispered explanation.

"We've got to hide this box somewhere."

"*She's* back again—in the drawing room with *him*," Gladys said scornfully. "But we won't take any chances. We'll go up the back stairs."

The children entered into the plan as though it were a game and slipped upstairs quietly. Rachel and Gladys followed them into the schoolroom.

"I *knew* Allan wasn't a thief," Dede said importantly.

"Me, too," piped up Ricky. "He was my friend."

Rachel handed Gladys the box. "Hide this in one of the cabinets; push it way to the back. I'm going to check to see how many of these are missing."

The suppressed air of excitement was contagious. Rachel again pledged the children to secrecy and left them with Gladys to go down the hall to where the Lalique collection was displayed. Rachel put her face close to the glass and peered inside. She saw that some of the crystal pieces had been moved to the front of the shelves to conceal the fact so many were missing. A clever ruse. There was no question now in Rachel's mind. This theft had been deliberate and premeditated. Planned! A few at a time so as not to be easily missed.

She must get word to Tony.

Gladys had to be brought into the picture. She was all too willing to help. She took the note downstairs and passed it to Melton. While Rachel was reading the children their bedtime story, Gladys came in.

"I'll take over for you, miss, if you like." She raised her eyebrows significantly. As Rachel handed her the book, Gladys slipped her a note.

"The maze, 8 p.m."

Rachel had to overcome her aversion to the hedged enclosure, especially at night. Her information was too important to let squeamishness hold her back.

"Good girl!" Tony declared when he heard what she had to tell him. "I'm taking the late train tonight to London. I'll see Inspector Sinclair first thing in the morning and give him this." He put the folded papers with the copied signatures in his vest pocket. "I'll tell him about the stolen Lalique. Maybe, he's got something more. Rachel, I'm sure we're close to finding out what happened to the *real* Verdonia Templeton."

Rachel lay awake long that night, her mind much too stimulated for her to sleep. Facing tomorrow was daunting. "Try to act as natural as possible," Tony had told her. "Don't give her the slightest hint you know the Lalique is missing or what we suspect. Nabbing this pair depends on surprise. They're clever and could get away before we have all the proof."

Rachel went over and over their hurried conversation, repeating it to herself. Most of all, she remembered the last thing Tony said to her, "You're wonderfully brave, Rachel." Then he had kissed her. She hoped, whatever tomorrow held, she could live up to his words.

A London Hospital

Sitting on the edge of her bed waiting for Dr. Spencer to make his ward rounds, she felt an anxiety attack coming on and clenched her hands more tightly in her lap. She tried to suppress the frightening wave of panic rising in her.

They told her to quell the attacks she had—to exert willpower, divert herself. But trying only seemed to add to her stress. Ironically, they told her just the opposite about her memory. She must not force it. Gradually, it would all come back—who she was, where she came from, where she had been going when the accident happened.

It was all so confusing.

She heard Dr. Spencer's hearty voice entering the ward, talking to patients in that annoyingly cheerful manner. At last he stood in front of her cubicle, Nurse Rogers behind him, her fixed smile in place.

"Well, now," he began, flipping open the patient chart. "Matron tells me you're about ready to go."

"I don't feel ready at all."

"Now, you can't stay here forever. You've been here nearly two months as it is. There is no valid reason for us to keep you any longer. We have many patients in much worse straits than you, my dear. There were others far more critically injured than you pulled from that wreck. I could tell you cases of mangled limbs, amputations that—" He shook his head. "Some did not survive. *You* ought to be grateful to be alive."

She sensed his rebuke and felt guilty.

"Other than a severe concussion, you suffered only a few broken ribs and a fractured wrist. There's no permanent damage."

"Except that I don't know who I am."

The doctor's cheerful expression faded. "The part of your brain that controls memory is simply not functioning—at least not yet. But that's only temporary. You'll just have to be patient."

He spoke to her as he might to a child. She jutted out her chin, gritted her teeth, and glared at him. The doctor didn't seem to notice, just went on talking.

"As soon as you're around familiar people and places, it will come back quickly enough."

Stupid man! How could that happen when she didn't know where any such familiar people or places might be? Dr. Spencer wrote something on the chart. She was sure it was his official order to dismiss her from this place. Such as it was, it was the place she had at least felt safe, sheltered, protected from some unknown evil, one she could not even name. She shuddered. Feeling the fear was about to take over again, she dragged her attention back to what Dr. Spencer was saying. "Now, let's see what they have here." Dr. Spencer consulted his chart. "Your general health is good. You're a little underweight, but that's only natural. You'll pick up in time. We know your age to be about forty, that you've had excellent nutrition all your life from the rapid way your bones healed, the condition of your skin, hair, and nails. Your teeth are—"

"I just have a brain that won't work," she interrupted tartly.

"You are well off financially," he said crossly. "So much better than many, many others."

She felt reprimanded. She knew what the doctor meant. She had been told that when they had undressed her after she was brought into the hospital, a money belt containing several hundred-pound notes was found under her clothes.

"Please spare me, doctor," she said wearily. What did the money really matter when she did not know where to go? Maybe she wasn't destitute, but she was certainly homeless.

Dr. Spencer finished whatever he was writing on her chart, closed his folder, sighed, gave her an exasperated look, and with a wave of his hand moved on to the next patient's bed.

"You'll be fine, dearie," the nurse said encouragingly. "As the doctor said, it will just take time."

"That's all right for *you* to say," she replied, then bit her trembling lower lip. She was sick of all of them, with their false assurances, their pat phrases. What did they really care? It was not their lives that had been lost. It was *hers!*

The nurse did not answer. Instead she opened the locker beside the bed and took out some clothes, asking brightly, "Are we ready to get dressed, then?"

181

"*You* appear to be sufficiently clothed. It is I who needs to get dressed."

Without another word, the nurse laid the clothes on the bedside, went out of the cubicle, and drew the curtains around it as she did.

Left alone, she examined the outfit curiously. They told her the clothes removed from patients brought in from the accident had all been cleaned and pressed. These seemed new but not the kind of traveling outfit she thought quite appropriate. Still, how could she say? She had no remembrance of what her taste in fashion might have been before the accident.

She went to the mirror over the washstand and put on the hat. She frowned. It looked odd. Not her style at all. How did she know that? She couldn't remember buying it. But then she couldn't remember much of anything else either.

For a moment she regarded her image gravely. It was like looking at a stranger. Is this who she was, before the accident had wiped out all memory of herself? The face was a pale oval. Clear gray eyes stared steadily back at her; a few strands of dark hair curled around her ears.

At the age they said she must be, she must have seen herself hundreds of times in dozens of mirrors. Why didn't she remember who she was?

She turned away with a sinking heart. Would she ever know? Would she ever return to the life she had left somewhere?

She walked down the ward, through the row of beds on either side, and out into the hospital corridor. She stopped at the desk.

The charge nurse handed her an envelope. "These are your valuables. We put them in the hospital safe for you. If you'd like to check them . . ."

Inside was a lady's fob watch, one broken earring with a peculiar stone, a thin gold chain. Nothing of value. Nothing to spark a memory. Had these been gifts or had she—whoever she was—bought them herself? She put them back in the envelope. Then she took out the watch and pinned it on her lapel. Although, what could time mean to her now?

Dr. Spencer came up to sign her out of the hospital, officially discharge her from his care.

"Well, I'll say good-bye then, and good luck," he said heartily.

"I shall need it," she replied solemnly.

A great deal of it, she thought, as she walked outside.

She stood for a minute at the top of the steps leading down into the busy London street. A cold damp wind hit her, and she shivered.

She was thin, too thin, and the light wool coat was not warm enough for the early fall evening. She swayed slightly, put out one hand to the iron railing to steady herself. She had told them she didn't feel ready to leave yet. But they hadn't listened.

Now what? Where should she go? She had money, she remembered. She walked down the rest of the steps to the curb, weakly she held up her arm, hailing one of the hansom cabs parked at the other end. It pulled up, and the driver leaned down from his seat and asked, "Where to, miss?"

"The Claridge Hotel."

Once seated in the leather interior, she wondered how she had known that name.

She stared out at the ocean. *How long have I been here? Weeks? Months?* Time seemed to have no meaning. She seemed to have come here midsummer. She couldn't be sure. The weather in this small coastal town was changeable. Day after day she had walked to the esplanade from the small seaside inn where she was staying, walked its length out to where the stone jetty projected itself, stood there feeling the salt spray on her face, watching the waves dash themselves up against the rocks, asking herself the same questions over and over. *What shall I do? Where shall I go? Where do I belong? And the last, most painful, unanswerable one—who am I?*

At the hospital it had even been speculated from her accent she could be a Canadian or perhaps an American. But even if that were true, she had no idea how and why she came to be in England. She shivered. How could that be? Every trace of her life before waking up in the hospital had been wiped away.

It was devastating. Depressing. Yet, down deep, she knew Dr. Spencer was right. She was better off than many. That is, until the money ran out. Then what? Shuddering, she turned around and walked back to the bench where she would sit for hours until the wind off the water turned cold, have tea, then return to the inn, go to her room, to bed, hoping to sleep. Seeking oblivion.

But there was a core of strength within her that would not let her give up. Not completely. There must be answers to her questions. Be patient, the doctor had counseled. Eventually, it will all come back. She looked down at her hands—no rings. She rubbed the third finger of her left hand. There was no ridge that might have been there from a wedding band. Her age was about forty. If she had been married, had children, wouldn't she somehow know that? She sighed.

Her common sense had led her here. After leaving the hospital she had stayed one miserable night at the Claridge Hotel, unable to sleep, in a state of confusion worse than she had experienced since first regaining consciousness. In the morning she'd had breakfast, then taken a cab to Harrods, bought a suitcase, a few basic items—underwear, stockings, a suit, some shirtwaists, a coat. She had changed in the ladies' lounge, neatly folded the clothes she had been wearing, and thrust them in a waste receptacle. Somehow they weren't right. She felt better in the new ones she had selected. Then she took another cab to Victoria Station, bought a train ticket to Craigburne. All this she did in a kind of automaton manner, propelled not so much by decision or choice, but by some kind of inner direction. It seemed the most logical thing to do. If anything was logical in her present condition.

The ticket stub found in one of her pockets had Craigburne stamped on it as her destination. Dr. Spencer had suggested that since it was not a large town, perhaps it would not be difficult to find out if she had friends or relatives there and had been on her way to visit them. Perhaps being there, the familiarity of the place, people, or surroundings might trigger her memory. Maybe someone there would recognize her, be able to identify her and help her discover her memory and identity. She had not had much hope but it was the only chance she had.

When the train had pulled into Craigburne and she got off, nothing looked familiar. Bewildered and depressed, she asked for a place to stay. The man at the ticket counter told her there were a few boardinghouses and one hotel, the Harbor Inn. He recommended it as it provided inexpensive, clean, attractive rooms, wholesome plain food. From the train station it was only a short distance, and she walked up the cobblestone street to the inn, a white plaster and timber building with bay windows facing the ocean. Inside it was furnished simply. Wicker furniture and faded flowered chintz gave it a comfortable, homey atmosphere. As she approached, a pleasant-faced woman behind the reception desk regarded her with kindly eyes.

She asked about renting a room and was told they had a very nice one on the second floor with an ocean view.

"I'll take it."

"Wouldn't you like to see it first?"

Realizing that must be the usual way of doing things, she almost panicked. "No, I'm sure it will be fine."

The woman turned the guest register book for her to sign, and for another moment, she felt trapped. Impulsively, she wrote Rose Baker. The name had suddenly flashed into her mind. Later she realized she had taken *Rose* from a soap wrapper and the surname from tinned cookies labeled Baker's Tea Biscuits, seen in a food shop. At least she had given herself a name, she thought, with some ironic humor.

She rented a room, paying a month in advance. Why not? Where else had she to go? And something just *might* happen. But so far nothing had, and each day she lost a little more hope. It was all so unnerving. Not knowing. Not sure. Not even remembering the awful train wreck that had brought her to this present condition. Every day she walked out, going into shops, strolling along the esplanade near the ocean, hoping someone might speak to her or seem to know her.

Craigburne was small, hardly more than a coastal village, populated mostly by fishermen and their families and temporary residents. The bracing sea air was thought to be healthful, and she sometimes saw people pushing invalid chairs. Others, not so obviously physically impaired, were perhaps seeking a respite from the bustle, noise, and dirt of London. It was a place of restoration from physical illness. But would it restore memory?

As she walked or sat on the benches along the esplanade, she watched other strollers, wondering if they were as lost and lonely as she felt. There were a few other guests at the inn she knew by sight, but they stayed only for a weekend or a few days, and she never exchanged more than a *good morning* or *good day* with anyone. She began to form certain habits. Like having her tea every afternoon in the cozy little tea shop not far from the hotel.

Today was warm, and whitecaps danced on the sun-sparkled water. It was just about time for tea, but she decided to sit and enjoy the sunshine for awhile. Leaning against the back of the bench, she closed her eyes, relishing the fresh, salty air. She was beginning to feel remarkably well, strong. If only . . . the same old restlessness seized her. *This can't go on indefinitely. I must find some way to discover who I am.*

Her inner resolve was interrupted by a quiet male voice. "Mind if I join you?"

She opened her eyes. A man was standing in front of her, momentarily blocking the sun. Squinting up at him, she recognized him as a fellow guest at the hotel. Although she didn't know his name, they had a nodding acquaintance. He was already at the inn when she arrived. While other guests had come and gone, he had remained. They saw each other every day in the small dining room, passed each other on the stairs or in the halls, greeted each other daily in passing as they both walked along the esplanade.

"Not at all." She straightened up, moved over to give him room to sit down.

"Although we haven't been formally introduced, as fellow guests at the inn, I felt it would be all right to speak. I'm Richard Holmes. My holiday is over, and I'm returning to London tomorrow."

For some reason, she felt a sharp pang of disappointment. He had become familiar to her. She had become used to seeing him every day, welcomed his friendly smile, his pleasant manner, his open, kind face. He had been a constant in a world that was otherwise unstable and frightening.

"You're leaving?"

"Yes. I cannot think of another excuse to stay." He smiled. "I must get back or lose my job completely." He spoke casually, as though that were not too important a consideration.

She gave him a discreet glance. He was nice looking close up. She had noticed before he was of medium build, with sandy hair liberally mixed with gray. He had an air of solid, middle-class prosperity about him. Today he was wearing a tweed Norfolk jacket over a beige roll-neck sweater. She noted he seemed to have benefited from his time here. When she first saw him, he appeared rather haggard and pale. Now his strong-featured face had color, and his intelligent eyes were bright.

He sighed and looked out at the ocean shimmering in the brilliant sun. "I hate to go. I shall miss all this—very much." He paused. "When I came here I was too weary to appreciate or really enjoy it. That's the trouble with most of us. We get too caught up in our lives—reaping, sowing, and spinning—to notice what really counts." He looked for her agreement, smiling. "Sometimes it takes a blow of some sort to make us stop and look and *really* see, to 'consider the lilies of the field.'"

His words struck a chord. As if she somehow recognized his reference. But how did she know that? She couldn't remember anything else either—not having sat on a bench in the middle of the day simply relishing the sun, the bracing salt air, the sheer beauty of things—nothing.

"Forgive me if I presume," he said gently. "Would it be too forward of me to ask if you'd join me for tea? A kind of farewell, a nice memory to take back to work with me. Will you do me the honor of being my guest for tea?"

She could think of no reason to refuse such a gracious invitation. What harm to share a pleasant interlude with the only other human being she had had contact with in—how long? Forever, it seemed.

"That would be nice. That is most kind of you."

"My pleasure." He smiled, and his lined face lighted up.

Within a few minutes they were seated in the alcove window of a tea shop with an ocean view. He ordered tea, crumpets, currant scones, and apricot jam.

"I must say being here has done me a world of good. When I came, I was at a low ebb. I'd just returned from India, and my health had been badly damaged by climate, illness—"

"India? Are you in the army?" she asked, wondering why that question came to mind at the word India.

"No, I'm a journalist. I was there to cover a story. I should have taken a rest after I returned, but something happened. A story I could not resist, and I overtaxed my strength more than I realized. That is why this has been such a great thing for me to get completely away for awhile."

"What kind of story couldn't you resist?"

He smiled a little sheepishly. "Like an old fire horse at the sound of the fire bell! It was a train wreck—actually not far from here—on the overpass coming across the trestle—some mix-up in signals. No one is sure of the real cause of the accident, but it was a terrible smash—cars derailed and overturned, lots of casualties, people still not accounted for.

"I had a relapse while I was doing the story, the preliminary investigation, so turned my notes and information over to a colleague—" He halted. "What is it? Have I said something to upset you?"

She shook her head, replacing her cup onto its saucer with a shaky hand. She leaned toward him across the table, her hands clenched tightly together. "No—it's just that—I have something to tell you, then maybe you can help me?"

21

The boy from the village news seller cycled up the long gravel drive around to the back, the tradesmen's entrance. He took out the London papers he now delivered daily to Talisman, placed them on the kitchen doorstep, then went whistling cheerily on his way.

In the butler's pantry, Melton set up Verdonia's breakfast tray. From the kitchen, Gladys brought in the plate of eggs, sausage, lamb chops, tomatoes, and triangles of toast, then covered it all with the domed silver warmer, measured four spoonfuls of tea into the small china pot, and carried everything into the pantry.

Melton was just about to put the newspaper into the slot on the side of the tray when a woman's photograph caught his eye. Melton turned and held out the paper so he could see it better.

A woman suffering from amnesia has come forward seeking help from any source to discover her true identity. A victim of the terrible train wreck near Craigburne early this summer, she remembers little of what happened before the collision.

She has some memory of being assaulted and robbed immediately before the two engines collided, resulting in the disastrous accident. Police are showing her pictures of women with criminal records in their files from which she hopes to identify her assailant. Below is the artist's composite sketch drawn from the victim's description of the woman as best she can remember. Police suspect whoever committed this crime may now be assuming this woman's identity.

Melton and Gladys scrutinized the sketch of the alleged assailant, then stared speechlessly at each other.

In a London rooming house, Leo Erwin woke up with a booming hangover. His head felt like a balloon. He'd made quite a night of it—celebrating. And there'd been something to celebrate. The money he'd received for the last lot was a surprise. Who'd have thought it was worth that much? Looked like some pretty ordinary glass to him. Well, it had all turned out better than he might have supposed.

Funny thing, Wyn showing up a few months ago like she had—out of thin air, you might say. Running into her at the train station after all those years. Looked uncommonly good, even though she must be close to forty-five. Had on a rakish hat, seemed chipper enough for all she'd been through. Said she was on her way to join a repertory troupe traveling the provinces. A long ways from what she might have had if it hadn't been for the scandal. Wyn Spencer might have been a star. Must've been about sixteen when Leo first met her.

She'd been a stunner then. Red hair, big eyes, pretty figure. Billed with a troupe of acrobats in their music hall days. A headliner she was then. Posters of her doing stunts. Quite an attraction. Leo remembered how young fellas from Oxford and Cambridge used to fill the seats, clapping enthusiastically whenever Wyn appeared on stage. A lot of stage door Johnnies they were, sending her bouquets of flowers, mash notes.

He could've told her she'd get into trouble. Mixin' with them young blue bloods. But she had ideas. Didn't take his advice. Too clever by half. A prank pulled off by some hot-head young university fellows for a lark. A bungled robbery. Quite a to-do. Their gentry parents got them off. But Wyn's picture and name were splashed all over the tabloids. Just the sort of thing those journals went for. Scantily-clothed, pretty young acrobatic star. An accessory. She'd foolishly worn some of the bangles they'd stolen and given to her. Served a short term in women's prison. When she came out, her music hall career was done for.

Wyn disappeared for a while. Laid low, he figured, until she thought it safe. Then she'd come back to London look-ing for work. Any kind of work. He'd used her in a couple of small jobs. She was a bit of an actress, could change her looks, put on accents. But she weren't too dependable. Had a mind of her own. She'd got caught shoplifting and was known to the police. He'd dropped her for awhile.

It was funny running into each other like they had. Wyn was bold as brass, made some joke about being a bad penny showing up. He'd wished her luck, and she'd had some. Bad luck. At least that's what it looked like at first. The train wreck.

He couldn't have been more surprised when a few weeks later he'd heard from her. She said she'd a proposition for him. She'd run into a gold mine. If he'd help her, he'd have a cut. Told him where she was, how to get there. If he was look-ing for a sure thing, a *main chance*, this was it.

Once he saw the place he knew she was right. Then she ex-plained—the woman on the train, the mix-up in identification.

All in all, he was glad she'd contacted him. Before Wyn had come back into his life, he'd had a long dry spell himself, that's for sure. Once they'd fenced the rest of the stuff, they could go their separate ways. Still, she was good enough company, and it had been as easy as taking candy from a baby.

Leo yawned and stretched. He dressed groggily, then walked out through the foggy morning to the nearby pub where he got some hair of the dog and then a mug of coffee and a bun. At the corner newsstand he picked up the morning paper, tucked it under his arm. He'd read it while he ate his breakfast, before going to the station to catch his train.

At the counter he greeted the waitress who filled his thick mug with steaming beverage and placed a scone studded with sultanas on a small plate. Leo carried them over to his regular table and took a long satisfying sip of coffee before opening his paper.

At the sight of the photograph and headline—*Do You Know This Woman?*—followed by the story of an amnesiac victim of the Craigburne train wreck, Leo nearly choked. He put down his mug with such force some of it spilled, scalding his fingers. He swore, read the article once more, then scraping back his chair, got to his feet and left without eating his bun.

At Talisman, in spite of Rachel's inner nervousness and apprehension, the morning went forward on its regular schedule. It was the day for the children's horseback riding lessons. Rachel took them down to the stable where their instructor waited. He was teaching them to jump, and low hurdles were placed around the riding ring. The ponies were brought out and saddled, and the children mounted. While they practiced, Rachel leaned on the rail watching, but her mind was in turmoil.

Was Tony in London? Had he met with Inspector Sinclair? Did they have enough evidence to go to the police? And what had happened to Mr. Venable's sister-in-law? Had she been kidnapped? Or *murdered?* Rachel shuddered.

When she had come to Talisman five months earlier, she could never have imagined this drama.

When the hour's lesson was over, Dede was ready to go back to the house with Rachel, but Ricky wanted to stay at the stables to help curry, groom, and feed the ponies.

"Do you know yet who stole Mama's crystal, Rachel?" Dede asked, as they walked to the house.

"Not yet, but I'm sure we will soon. Your Uncle Tony is working hard to find out."

When they entered the house, no one was around, but as they started upstairs, they heard loud voices furiously raised. Exchanging a glance, they crept the rest of the way up the stairs to the top. They recognized Gladys's voice, then Verdonia's distorted with anger.

Rachel leaned down and whispered, "Dede, I must see what all this is about. Run down to the schoolroom like a good girl. Lock the door and stay there until I come and get you. Promise?"

The little girl nodded and ran down the hall.

Rachel hurried toward Verdonia's suite at the other end. The sitting room door was wide open, but the Chinese screen in front of it half concealed the hall. There was no mistaking the fierce confrontation going on between the two women.

"How dare you accuse me!" Verdonia demanded.

"Because I seen the evidence with me own eyes!" Gladys shouted back. "What do you call what you're puttin' in that bag?"

"How dare you call me a thief!"

"A thief you are, and probably worse! A murderer maybe." Gladys snatched up the newspaper from the floor, where it had fallen out of Verdonia's lap when she had leaped to her feet at Gladys's entrance. "What did you do to the *real* Miss Verdonia Templeton, that's what I'd like to know!"

Involuntarily, Rachel shrank back as she saw Verdonia's arm swing back then forward, dealing Gladys such a hard slap it staggered the girl. Momentarily dazed by the blow, Gladys lunged at Verdonia with both hands and gave her a violent push. Verdonia stumbled backward onto the chaise lounge.

Impulsively, Rachel started to rush to Gladys's aid, when all of a sudden she heard footsteps on the stairway and turned to see Leo Erwin coming up, taking the steps two at a time. Without even taking time to wonder how he got into the house or why he was here and in such a hurry, Rachel slipped behind the Chinese screen, hiding herself.

"Wyn! Wyn!" Leo shouted in a rasping voice as he thundered down the hall.

Wyn? What did that mean?

"What the devil's going on!" he demanded, stopping at the threshold of the sitting room.

Through the space between the folding panels Rachel saw the husky country girl struggle against the surprising strength of the erstwhile invalid.

At the sight of Leo standing dumbfounded at the door, Verdonia shouted, "Don't stand there like a fool! Come help me. Grab this wildcat!"

Leo rushed in and grabbed Gladys, dragged her away, twisting one of her arms behind her.

"What's this all about? Look, Wyn, the game's up. Verdonia Templeton's picture is plastered all over London, in the newspapers and in posters on lampposts and buildings. Big black letters asking *Do You Know This Woman?* and under that, *Notify Scotland Yard!* We gotta get out of here. Fast. Where's the loot?"

Wyn's face blanched. "Most of it's packed. I was just getting some of it when *she*—"

"Never mind that. What do you want me to do with her? We can't let her go till we bolt, or she'll blab to—"

"You bet your sweet life I will," Gladys taunted. "Melton went to report you to the police. They'll be here any minute to arrest you two and put you where you belong."

"Shut up!" Verdonia snarled.

Rachel wanted to help Gladys, but her better sense stopped her. If she made her presence known, she could easily be overpowered by both of them. That wouldn't help Gladys. Best to remain hidden. Watch, see what they did. Then act.

Her main concern was the children. Dede was safe enough if she remained where she was. But Ricky might come running in at any minute. Not knowing what was happening he could be grabbed by Leo, used as a hostage. Who knew what this evil couple were capable of? Whatever happened, at whatever cost, she had to protect the children. Risking *her* life wouldn't help them.

She listened as Leo said, "Pay attention, Wyn. I've got a hired hack outside waiting to take us to the station. If we hurry, we can get the next train to London, then from there to Liverpool, catch the boat to France. But there's no time to waste. What about the girl?"

Gladys was still struggling, and Leo tightened his grip, causing her to give a yelp of pain.

"Get something to gag her with," Leo ordered. "We'll have to put her somewhere till we're safely gone."

Rachel winced, watching him pull Gladys across the floor toward the closet. The maid was still valiantly kicking and squirming.

"Come on, Wyn, get that door open so we can shove her in fast," Leo said, panting from exertion.

Wyn, breathing heavily, brushed back a strand of hair that had fallen in her face. "I left a bag of the crystal stuff in the maze. Did you pick it up?"

"No! We've no time to waste. Besides we got enough loot. I fenced it for a good price. Too bad there's still a fortune here to be took, but we'll have to leave it.

"Come on! No telling who else has seen that paper."

Together they pushed Gladys inside the closet and slammed the door. Leo took a chair and wedged the back of it under the door handle. He adjusted his jacket sleeves, then he turned and saw Wyn stuffing the silver dresser set into a pillow sham, emptying the contents of the jewelry box into it as well.

"Didn't you hear what I said, woman?" he yelled. "The local paper might just pick up the story. It might be only a matter of hours before the local constabulary is alerted. How long do you think it'll be before somebody puts two and two together? You'll be arrested!"

"For what?" she demanded. "They can't prove anything. I had a concussion, remember? I might not have known who I was either."

"Well, I do, and you're pretty stupid if you don't know you'll be in a far worse pickle if we don't get out of here and fast." Leo was yelling, his voice edgy.

"All right, all right! Here, you take this." She thrust the bulging pillowcase at him. "Go ahead, I'm right behind you. Just want to get a few more things."

Rachel flattened herself against the wall, scarcely daring to breathe. She glanced around frantically. How could she stop the thieves and rescue Gladys? Suddenly her gaze fell on the twin Moorish statues. She reached for one, lifted it, feeling its weight as she did. Quickly she stepped back behind the screen. As Leo started out of the room, Rachel raised the heavy figurine and with all her might brought it down on his head. Groaning, he fell to the floor, dropping the bag, spilling the stolen contents all over the polished floor.

Looking down at the man's crumpled body, Rachel saw blood spurt from the back of his head, and her stomach lurched. She had never struck anyone before in her entire life, much less with such force and such murderous intent. For a moment she felt paralyzed by what she had done. Had she killed him? Even as that thought traumatized her momentarily, his leg twitched, his hand clenched then unclenched, and she knew he was still alive.

Hearing loud banging from where Gladys had been imprisoned, Rachel sprang into action. She dashed into the room, over to the closet, and wrenched the chair away from under the closet doorknob. But before she could turn it to free Gladys, she heard a howling behind her and felt a hard thump on her back. Hands clutched her shoulders, trying to pull her away from the closet door. But it was too late. Gladys had kicked the door open and was sliding on her hands and knees into the room.

Wyn screamed wildly as she clawed at Rachel, who was now straining to get away from her. Rachel heard cloth tearing. Her bodice was ripped from the seam of the sleeve and torn away. With a handful of torn cloth, Wyn lunged at Rachel again, but this time, Gladys was on her feet beside Rachel, and they both pummeled her.

Losing her balance, Wyn stumbled back against the sofa, reaching out for the small table beside it, which toppled over, sending a crystal vase of flowers crashing and splintering into dozens of pieces. She fell back onto the chaise lounge, and Gladys grabbed one of her arms and yanked her up and to her knees. Gladys was upon her in a minute, pushing her to the floor by sitting on her back.

Curses mingled with moans, and vicious name-calling emanated from the prone woman until Gladys reached behind her for a sofa pillow and plunked it over the woman's head, stifling the sounds. Then, flushed and disheveled she looked up at Rachel triumphantly and gave a broad wink.

Panting hard, Rachel leaned on the back of a chair, in total disbelief of the melee in which she had been involved.

"Better get sumpin and tie him up—just in case!" Gladys directed. "Though from the looks of things, I don't think he's goin' anywhere. Melton should be here afore long. He went to the village police soon as we saw the morning paper and wuz able to put two and two together."

"The morning paper?" Rachel stared at her blankly. "What do you mean?"

"That's right, you don't know." Gladys pointed with her thumb to the woman upon whom she was sitting. "This here is an impostor." Gladys seemed pleased with her use of the word. "The *real* Verdonia Templeton lost her memory. She's been in a London hospital and in Craigburne, trying to figure out who she is."

"But how—" Rachel began.

Gladys shook her head, shrugging her plump shoulders.

"Don't know exactly how it happened—some kind of royal mix-up when the injured was taken out of the train wreck. Looks like this one just decided to take advantage of the doctors makin' a mistake in identifying her. They took her for Miss Templeton."

Dazed by what she was hearing, Rachel simply shook her head in bewilderment. Then she thought of the children. She must go see that they were all right. But first she had to secure the other prisoner. She yanked the tasseled cord from the draperies and tied Leo's hands behind him.

He groaned and twisted his head around as she pulled hard on the knot. "Take it easy, you near broke me arm. My head's killin' me. I could file charges agin you for assault."

Rachel made no response, just pulled harder on the cord as she crossed his ankles and tied them. With a protesting moan, he put his head down again.

"I must see to the children," Rachel told Gladys. "Can you hold out here for a few minutes?"

"That I can."

Rachel started out of the room. Just as she reached the hall, she heard the sound of booted footsteps marching up the stairs. She entered the hallway just in time to see Melton accompanied by two uniformed policemen and followed by Tony.

"Are you all right?" Tony came toward her.

All she could do was nod. "Fine. Thank God you're here."

"Inspector Sinclair is on his way, and a man from Scotland Yard as well. I think we've just about solved the case, Rachel. We've located the *real* Verdonia Templeton. I've seen her myself, talked to her. She's still awfully confused, but what happened on the train before the wreck is coming back to her." His mouth straightened into a grim line. "And that woman in there—" They could hear Verdonia viciously swearing at the policemen. "She has a lot to answer for."

The next few minutes became a blur in Rachel's mind. The two policemen took charge of Leo and the woman they called Wyn Spencer and soon left. Melton had gone to them immediately upon seeing the story in Verdonia's London morning paper. They had already been alerted by Inspector Ross Sinclair and were checking with Scotland Yard regarding apprehending the two.

It was much later that Rachel and Tony had a chance to piece everything together, unraveling the whole of the mysterious events at Talisman.

The following afternoon, sitting on the terrace, Tony shook his finger playfully at Rachel. "And *you* a vicar's daughter, tch, tch," he teased. "You landed quite a wallop on Leo Erwin's head. He complained about it all the way into London."

"Desperate circumstances demand desperate measures," Rachel said archly, smiling.

"Spare me your quotations. I believe you make half of them up anyway."

"Not at all. I want to hear the rest of what you and Inspector Sinclair found out about Verdonia—*both* Verdonia and Wyn Spencer."

They were sitting together on the garden bench in the sun-dappled autumn afternoon. As if on cue, they both turned to look out to where the children were walking, holding the hands of a tall, slender woman. Their Aunt Verdonia Templeton, newly arrived at Talisman.

"Well, my suspicions were aroused almost from the beginning. She was so different in so many ways from the Verdonia Templeton I remembered. But I kept telling myself my youthful memory could be fuzzy. I think it was after Inspector Sinclair's visit that I developed a strong conviction the woman was not who she said she was. The question was how could I prove it? I guess Sinclair suspected her from the day he brought down the luggage. He's trained to detect lies, and there was something evasive about her responses. Not being able to give the slightest information about anyone else being in the compartment she shared with the *real* Verdonia."

"I wish you'd told me. I had my own misgivings about her, but they were based on my observation. Never having met the *real* lady, I attributed her strangeness to the injuries from the train wreck."

"Until I was sure, I figured the less you knew, the less you would give away. That's why I contacted Melton. He told me about the missing valuables, that Allan had been dismissed and Mrs. Coulter left. He also had met the *real* Verdonia Templeton and would have a better idea of how the two women differed. But finally, it was Verdonia herself who actually broke the case."

"How do you mean?" Rachel asked.

"First by agreeing to the controversial method of restoring her memories. Mesmerism is still considered experimental, you know. But she was willing to undergo it. That took courage. It worked, in her case. She remembered how Wyn pretended losing her first-class train ticket and how she offered to share her compartment with her, then the brutal physical assault when she caught Wyn rifling her suitcase, stealing her things. Then later she was brave enough to tell her story to the reporter, have it printed in the London papers. I admire her a great deal."

"She's certainly different from the Verdonia we thought had come to Talisman," Rachel said ruefully.

Tony glanced out to where the children and Verdonia strolled toward the maze. "Well, I guess you might say, all's well that ends well. The riddle is solved. Verdonia is here and quickly recovering her memory. Brett is on his way home."

The Australian papers had carried the bizarre story of the amnesiac and the woman who had taken her place. Brett Venable had cabled Talisman immediately and caught the next ship back to England.

"All of this will soon seem like a nightmare that never happened." Tony regarded Rachel with thoughtful eyes. "Your job here is almost over, Rachel. Any plans?"

"I haven't had time to catch my breath, much less think of the future."

"Now that the truth is coming out about everything, I'd like to know the truth of your feelings for me. Almost from the first, I've made mine about *you* quite clear, but I'm baffled about yours. Should I believe what I think I see in your eyes?"

So frankly confronted, Rachel could not pretend any longer. Her emotions had been in tumult for the last few days, knowing that with the return of Brett Venable her time at Talisman could be at an end. All her feelings were too near the surface. She turned her head so Tony could not see her sudden tears. She dreaded the thought of leaving the children, perhaps never seeing Tony again.

"What is it, Rachel?" Tony put his index finger under her chin, and slowly turned her averted head back so she had to meet his searching gaze. "Do you care for me? I have to know because I love you. So very much, my dearest."

She tried to find words, but there was no chance. Tony drew her to him, then softly kissed her. She closed her eyes, responding to his gentleness.

When she opened her eyes, Tony was smiling at her. She felt dazed and happier than ever she thought possible. So this was what all the poetry was written about, the meaning of all the sentimental songs. He kissed her again, slowly, and a warmth spread through her that she did not want to resist, nor could she.

When the kiss ended, Tony sighed happily. "Well, I guess I have my answer! Now, Miss Penniston, another important question. Will you marry me?"

"Marry?"

"Of course! We love each other. What could be more logical than to get married?"

"But—" She faltered. "There are problems."

"None that can't be solved. What do you see as a problem?"

"The disparity in our backgrounds, our social stations—"

"Nonsense," Tony scoffed. "Who cares about such things? I certainly don't! The only problem I can foresee is—" Here he frowned fiercely, his eyes clouded with uncertainty. "You might not want to live in Greece."

"Greece?"

"Yes. I'm being sent there as part of the embassy staff for at least two years. Would you mind?"

This was too much. It couldn't be true. Rachel felt laughter bubbling up inside her.

"You're *laughing!*" He looked bewildered. "Have I said something funny? Or is it at *me* you're laughing?"

Finally she found her voice. "It's unbelievable! What I mean is—and—I'm not laughing at you. I mean, *no* I wouldn't mind living in Greece. I'd love it!" She smiled at him, then pretended to frown. "Do you have any more secrets you're keeping from me?"

Tony looked serious, hesitated a moment. "Well, yes, perhaps I ought to tell you the deepest, darkest one. I write poetry. In fact, I've had several slim books of verse published—under another name."

Irrepressible laughter came again. Rachel could hardly believe her ears. All her wildly impossible dreams coming true? Her romantic, free-spirited lover, her poet ready to carry her away to live on a Greek isle, all here, in the person of the man with whom she had fallen so foolishly in love.